Haunting
Sunshine

Haunting Sunshine

Jack Powell

 Pineapple Press, Inc.
Sarasota, Florida

In memory of my father,
The Reverend Jack B. Powell, Sr.
He found and nurtured the good in all who knew him.

Inquiries should be addressed to:

Pineapple Press, Inc.
P.O. Box 3899
Sarasota, Florida 34230

www.pineapplepress.com

Library of Congress Cataloging in Publication Data

Powell, Jack, 1950–
     Haunting sunshine / by Jack Powell.— 1st ed.
cm.
     Includes bibliographical references (p.   ) and index.
     ISBN 1-56164-220-7 (pbk. : alk. paper)
   Haunted places—Florida.

   BF1472.U6 P69 2001
   133.1'09759—dc21

                                                        00-050215

First Edition
10 9 8 7 6 5 4 3 2 1

Photographs not credited were taken by the author
Design and production by *osprey*design
Printed in U.S.A.

Table of Contents

Acknowledgments

A number of people were so helpful in the writing of this book that I have to admit the good parts are from them and any mistakes must be from me. In gathering information and context, I am proud to have had the assistance of Jessi Jackson Smith and Dana Ste. Claire of the Daytona Museum of Arts and Sciences, Adrian Davis, Lynn Smallwood McMillin, Fr. Tryfon K. Theophilopolous, Paula Sackett of the Lake Worth Playhouse, the Reverend Paul Rasmus, Sonny Robinson, Virginia Jackson, Marty Hamrick, Anna and Douglas Gaidry, the Reverend James Taylor, Bob and Angie Clark, and Linda Spitzer. They all helped verify accuracy as well.

As I mooched and bummed across Florida, gracious hospitality was provided by John and Elizabeth Davis, Jade Siminitus, Sharon Hamrick, and Crystal Sirmans.

Most of the chapters were composed on Monday nights at Hops Microbrewery and Restaurant in Lakeland. Thanks to the staff for patiently delivering order after order of perfect ribs to me as I day-dreamed for hours in the back corner.

No ghosts were harmed in the composition and production of this book. Whenever there was any possibility of danger, medical students were used instead.

JBP
Bartow, Florida

Introduction

For the first forty-nine years of my life, I got along perfectly well with ghosts because we had no interest in each other. My attitude was "live and let live," if living was whatever it was that they were doing. I was busy slogging through school and pursuing a career in medicine. Later I retired, having served twenty years in the military as both a pediatrician and pediatric cardiologist. None of my military duties had involved ghosts. My career had been spent in keeping young people on my side of the line that separated the living from the spooks.

Retirement was brief. I spent much of my newly free time attending to household tasks that my lovely wife told me I wanted to do. The rest was spent in covering the practices of friends who needed a break for vacation or a medical meeting. An apartment was provided for me near the out-of-town hospital I worked at most frequently. The apartment was spacious, well furnished, conveniently located, and haunted.

Doctors who stayed overnight at the apartment often refused to stay there again. Lights blinked, people were pinched while supposedly alone, and apparitions were clearly seen. One person awakened to find herself pinned down in bed by something unseen, unable to move her arms or legs. When released a moment later, she ran into the living room where a friend had been sleeping on the couch. The same thing had just happened to him.

It was difficult to laugh off the stories as being from superstitious, unreliable people. These same people had successful pediatric practices. Each day they proved the reliability of their judgment and powers of observation. When I left work for the day, I was leaving the sickest children in the city in their care.

It was not long before I had some strange, but fortunately benign, experiences in the apartment. Knowing the biblical injunctions against consulting with mediums or witches, I asked some church leaders of different denominations whether a haunting was inherently evil. None thought so. One clergyman, a fundamentalist, laughed as he told me how much he enjoyed hearing or reading a good ghost story.

Soon afterwards I was recruited to Florida to set up a practice in a rural area that needed more physicians. I immediately began collecting Florida folklore and soon had a database that included about two hundred hauntings. The range was as colorful as Florida's past and present. These were stories of passion, adventure, devotion, revenge, and secrets. All were spiced with some degree of the unknown. They were from the shadowy border of Florida's history, where people whose names we know grappled with invisible forces that we still don't fully understand.

Some Floridians object to ghost stories and claim that the Bible condemns them as evil. They're wrong. I encourage these folks to inquire of their clergy about the subject as I did. Other people are quick to reassure me that they are not crazy enough to believe any of the stories. But is it necessary to believe them in order to enjoy them?

There are things to think about in the following pages, but mainly I hope that people enjoy reading the stories. Some parts are comical. Others are deliciously creepy in a tingly sort of way. Perhaps the best way to read this book is the same way that so many of us watched scary movies as children: by peeking through our fingers. Or maybe we should always leave the light on.

Haunting Sunshine

Stage Frights:
Haunted Theaters

Falk Theater

In the time of Bessie Snavely, the Falk Theater was not yet the Falk Theater. That would be later in the century. It was the 1930s, and the building in Tampa was known as the Park Theater. Built as a vaudeville house, it was home to a succession of touring companies.

Bessie Snavely was an actress whose dressing room was on the third floor. She was at an important moment in her career. Sadly, her husband was not there to share the moment with her. He had left her for a stagehand, but Bessie had gone on performing. Her name, as a faithful but wronged wife, was on everyone's lips. The irony was that her misfortune was great publicity. From Bessie's vantage point, the whole theater revolved around her. The walls of her dressing room turned about her slowly. After a few moments, they slowed, then stopped, then began rotating in the other direction. In reality it was Bessie who was turning, at the end of a noose.

Partly because one of their number had been involved, theater techies have been nervous about Bessie Snavely's dressing room for

University of Tampa's Falk Theater

decades. Most have avoided it when possible. Those who had to go in reported a coldness that went beyond any climate control. Some have reported a coldness elsewhere in the theater. Others have noticed a constant presence of something unseen but benign. Some just never feel truly alone in the theater, even when it is empty after hours.

One professor saw a set of dressing room doors opening and slamming shut by themselves, in rapid succession. Another staff member may have actually seen Bessie, or at least a manifestation of her.

"I was in my office and heard noises outside my door, which opens into the theater," he told me. "It sounded like a pounding. I got up and opened the door and looked where the noise was coming from. It stopped as soon as I opened the door. There was a mist there, like a white fog or luminous cloud, that was disappearing into the wall. It had no shape."

There are over fifty years of Bessie stories but none of them hostile. People have just had to accept that there are aspects of the theater that they can't control. Another staff member was on a scaffold doing some painting. He lost his balance and almost fell off. He was alive and unhurt and talked to me later. Something invisible had caught him and righted him on the scaffolding.

Was it Bessie? She gets the credit for some incidents in the theater. In taking her own life, she may have developed more of an appreciation for life itself. Whatever the answer, each production in the Falk Theater transports its audience to another world. One can only speculate what has been transported to our world.

Lake Worth Playhouse

F lorida ghosts often act as if they are good-natured, and they frequently indulge in pranks. Arthur of the Cassadaga Hotel and "Fatty" Walsh of the Biltmore are both good and well-known examples. But one might not anticipate the spirit of Lucien Oakley to manifest a sense of humor.

Lucien Oakley and his brother, when they built the Lake Worth Playhouse as a vaudeville house in 1924, were plagued by everything except good fortune.

The construction costs greatly overran the original estimates. Lucien Oakley supplied most of the money and even provided extra money for the construction. The damage done to his finances was exceeded only by the damage done to the building by a hurricane in 1928. The crash of the Florida land boom and development and then the stock market crash of 1929 eventually helped drive Lucien to kill himself. Popular legend has it that he hanged himself in the theater. The truth is that he shot himself at his home. Nevertheless, it's Lucien whose apparition has been occasionally seen at the playhouse.

It may be that he still feels a sense of responsibility toward the theater. New technicians feel a presence watching them for a while after they begin working there. As they become proficient at their tasks, the presence leaves. Some think that Lucien is acting as a sort

Lake Worth Playhouse

of supervisor, making sure that the new hands will work out all right.

Many incidents take place in the area of dressing rooms. One young actress heard her name called by a male voice; no one was there when she turned to look. Another person saw Oakley briefly in a mirror. Unexplained blasts of cold air used to occur, but are now confined just to dressing rooms.

Years ago, a giant handprint was seen by some on one wall of the theater. The print vanished, but people would come back day after day and find that heavy objects had been moved about by an unknown force. In recent years, Oakley's flair for the dramatic has lessened. The objects that move now are smaller, much lighter, and leave a trail.

The artists of the Lake Worth Playhouse have a rarely seen colleague who dabbles in a unique art form and occasionally puts on a little private show. Like children "rolling" a house, the specter of the Lake Worth Playhouse leaves his marks with toilet paper. Roll after roll will depart the restrooms and meander through the theater till completely unwound. The ghostly artist has even used several rolls to make patterns on the lobby floor.

Despite a tragic past, the ghost of Lucien Oakley entertains those who have come after him, and he watches over them. The footsteps that are heard from the empty catwalks above are the sounds of someone walking on wood. The catwalks are now all metal. Could Lucien be watching across time as well, from the wooden catwalks of decades long past?

Tampa Theatre

The most celebrated theater haunting in Florida is that of the grand old Tampa Theatre. Opened in 1926, this landmark has a long list of lavish and ornate features that today's suburban shoe boxes have never heard of. The theater is still used year-round. There are statues of mythological and historical figures, a sweeping ceiling with twinkling lights that resemble stars, fountains, and of course a Mighty Wurlitzer organ. With the statues, gargoyles, cherubs, and the building's vastness, one might expect that the theater could be a trifle spooky when it is darkened and supposedly empty. Fortunately, all the resident ghost seems to want to do is have fun. Unfortunately, that particular ghost has been watching movies and audiences for decades and knows just how to get a reaction.

Foster "Fink" Finley was a projectionist at the Tampa Theatre from 1930, four years after it opened, till 1965, when he died of a heart attack. He was part of the unseen mechanism that stayed in the background and made certain that the show went on. Although the theater might not open till one o'clock in the afternoon, he would arrive via bus at seven or eight o'clock in the morning, attired in suit and tie, and then change once he got to his projectionist's booth. The booth itself was small and cramped, filled with its projectors, two chairs, and a workbench. There was barely enough room for the two projectionists and the cigarette that was a permanent feature of one corner of Finley's mouth. Finley stayed there the whole time, making certain that his projector worked smoothly. He seemed perfectly content.

People could only take his word for it that he had a wife and a family, till the day in 1965 that he became ill in his booth. A coworker took him home and saw that he really did have a life other than the Tampa Theatre, though it hadn't seemed that way. Finley died two months later.

It was not long afterward that the theater staff began whispering among themselves that Foster Finley was as reliable as ever about showing up. Members of movie audiences reported seeing an apparition float across the screen during the films. Projectionists who were concentrating on the film, waiting for the cue to switch projectors, would hear the generator in a nearby room get louder, as if someone were opening the door precisely at the time the projectionist would not be able to turn around and look. When the switch had been made, the sound would become softer, and the door could be seen to be closed.

Foster Finley's heart attack had given him his first big break. He was now a star of stage and screen.

He had no problem with name recognition. Among the theater staff, he was a legend as part of the theater bedrock. The specifics of his pranks, including holding open the door of the projectionist's booth while the projectionist was trying to close it, ensured that people knew who was haunting them.

In death he did what he had never done in life, and that was to roam the theater itself. One worker left a men's room and felt a sensation of "a cold wind, but without the wind." He is certain that he accidentally walked right through Finley. People have seen a door open and close by itself, as if someone unseen had just come through it. A power switch once turned off, despite being well away from anyone present at the time.

A figure in white has been seen sitting in the theater when the building was supposed to be empty.

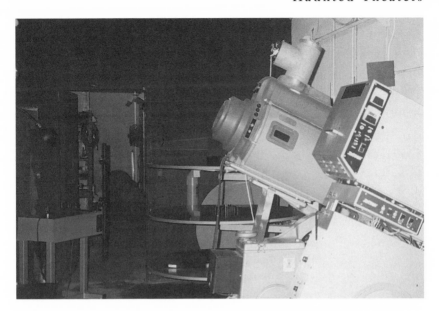

Tampa Theatre's projection booth; the door to the generator room is open in back

One worker felt himself being tapped on the same shoulder repeatedly while mopping the lobby. The same worker was on the third floor and found himself again and again turning off a shower, which would wait till he had left...then turn on again.

There were the usual manifestations, suggesting that Finley had mastered the basics of haunting. Objects seemed to move around by themselves. Something put down in one place would be found later some place else. One person carried a knife on his belt, but it had vanished. He searched for the knife for days while working throughout the theater. Remembering that someone had told him that ghosts would return an object if asked to do so, he asked aloud for the knife. He turned around, and the knife was on the floor, leaning against the wall of the projectionist's booth. It was in plain sight in an area that he had already searched several times.

Theaters being what they are, evidently Finley cannot resist the Hollywood touch. The jangling of keys that people have heard in the empty theater is just a warm-up. Standing outside the empty and locked building, the sounds of chains being slowly dragged across the floor inside may be heard. They have before. It's the only performance in the Tampa Theatre that is not announced by the Mighty Wurlitzer. It is the theater's longest-running performance. Admission is free. The star is Foster Finley. Show time? He'll let you know.

Center Place

The complex that represents the cultural center in Brandon also houses the library where I did a considerable amount of research into Florida's haunted places. The intellectual activity of one area spills over into the others—artwork adorns the library throughout. Brochures and posters lure one from one activity to another. Art classes for young and old can be enjoyed, as well as theater productions. The center is a good place to escape boredom. Even the tranquil surroundings outside the center make it a pleasure to be bored, if one is so inclined.

A girl who has been nicknamed Matilda (but whose real name may be Susan) gently haunts Brandon Center. Brandon Center stands on the former site of a funeral home. A young woman named Susan, who had been an artist, had been one of its "clients."

The first reported sighting of Susan was by a staff member who was answering a security call. An apparition of a shy young girl dressed in blue was seen near a Coke machine. The girl vanished quickly and could not be found upon a search of the premises. She has not been seen since, although people have sensed an unseen presence.

The most common manifestations have to do with the artwork throughout the center. Paintings move from one place to another without explanation. Frequently they are found hanging crookedly, as if they had been taken down and not put back very well. No damage has ever been done.

Susan may not just be a denizen of the night. Some reporters came to Brandon Center once to do a story on her. It was a beautiful day outside, with blue skies and no threat of bad weather. As the staff began talking about Susan, the lights flickered as if there were an electrical storm. The ideal weather outside continued. There were no other electrical problems in the building, not even with the computers. The flickering continued until the conversation about Susan was over and the reporters were preparing to leave.

Be it Susan or Matilda, the shy ghost of Brandon Center seems to be finding all she wants at Brandon Center. Perhaps one of the art classes should leave some supplies out for her to use. She might find the hint irresistible. The results could be fascinating!

Daytona Playhouse

Although I was two generations younger than my uncle John, who was taking me on a tour of his beloved Daytona Beach, I was pleased to note that both of us thought of the same things when we considered Daytona: the speedway, the beach, and the surf. We were both surprised when we drove into Daytona Beach from South Daytona Beach and saw the sign perched firmly on the median strip: "Welcome to Daytona Beach: Tree City, USA."

My uncle and aunt had lived in Daytona Beach, and I was a tourist, but none of us understood who the target audience of the sign was. We dutifully pulled over and admired the trees for a few moments. Then we continued the tour, working our way up the beach and meandering through some neighborhoods and along the Halifax River. Along the river is where you will find the Daytona Playhouse and other signs that Daytona Beach has permanent residents besides trees. In the Daytona Playhouse you will find a couple of ghosts.

The first sighting was in 1972. Unfortunately, it was during a performance. Fortunately, no one was hurt, though the actor who was hoisting his dancing partner to his shoulders lost his grip and nearly dropped her when he saw the transparent figure of a woman wearing a large plumed hat.

Other sightings have been before smaller audiences. Two women getting a set ready saw a short man with a moustache. He walked into a dressing room, ignoring their queries, and vanished when they followed him into the room. Except for the entrance door, there was no other exit that a human being could have used. Possibly the same male apparition has been seen sitting in the audience watching productions or hanging around the vicinity of dressing rooms. He is obvious because of his dapper 1930s-style clothing, with a scarf or a cape thrown across one shoulder.

Investigation shows no great tragedy in the playhouse, such as a death or a murder, that could have left a spectral residue—the aura or emotions left at the site where a person has died. There are stories of two lovers who lived in the area and who died tragic deaths: He died fighting in a war in Spain, and she committed suicide when she could wait for him no longer. She was pregnant. She drowned herself and their unborn child in the Halifax River.

Some believe that the ghosts are the two lovers. The problem is that the two spirits don't seem to be aware of each other. Manifestations of unknown forces continue—doors open and close and nothing comes through but a cool breeze. The story unfolds slowly, with the Daytona Playhouse as the set.

A Night at the Roxy

I don't think you've ever heard this story. It's not documented anywhere that I know of," said the roguish-looking but instantly likeable fellow facing me. We were sitting in the dining area of a house in Middleburg. It was nearly midnight. "You know the Roxy Theater in Jacksonville?"

I had never heard of it.

"It's gone now. I think there's a parking lot and an auto parts store where it used to be. Years and years ago it was a grand old theater, a real special place for people to go. They would have singing acts on stage and then show the latest movies. Then it went to burlesque. Around the fifties or sixties it was going downhill and getting crummy. I spent a summer working as a projectionist there. By that time it was showing porno flicks. There was a room next to the theater where there were peep shows. You went into a booth, pulled the curtains for privacy, and dropped in a quarter. Then you'd get a few minutes of whatever was on the cartridge in that booth. If you wanted more, you put in more quarters. Each booth had a different cartridge. I changed them once a week.

"Believe me, I wasn't into that stuff. But I needed a job, and it was okay money. The owner was always real nice to me. I got paid fair and on time. But there was strange stuff happening at the Roxy. It wasn't just me. Another guy who worked there after me had things happen to him too."

I asked him what.

"The bathroom doors. They were downstairs, below the projectionist's booth where I spent most of my time. They would open and close by themselves. It was never once—always two or three times. But the whole time I worked there, the hinges didn't work. They were rusted through. Those doors were hard to open or close. When no one was near them, they'd open by themselves and slam shut like the hinges worked perfectly, or something really strong was moving them.

"Like I said, I spent most of my time in the booth. There were two carbon-arc projectors up there. Each one would hold a reel about three feet wide, good for an hour of film. When the first reel was almost done, timing dots would appear on the corner of the screen. The dots showed a countdown to when I had to start the second reel. I didn't get next to the projectors until I had to. They were great projectors, but carbon-arc ones all get hot and they give off carbon monoxide. I'd stay in the back of the booth next to the window while the film was running, or work in the editing room off to the side.

"Sometimes I'd be sitting in the back of the booth and I'd hear voices. They weren't from the theater or the audience. They were coming from the editing room. There weren't any windows in that room—the only way in was just the door into it from the booth. I could tell that nobody was in there from where I was sitting."

I noted that at least it was nobody he could see.

"Right. I'd listen, but I could only make out a word every now and then. I could never quite figure out what they were saying. I felt like I was eavesdropping on a conversation."

I asked about the audience. Didn't it bother them?

"They never heard it. I'm not surprised. It was coming from the room right next to me, and I could barely hear it.

"I never saw anything except for those bathroom doors. I'd be down in the theater cleaning up after everybody had left. The doors would be closed…then I'd look up and they would be open, but I knew there was nobody around but me. I'd get scared, believe me. I'd leave the theater for the lobby and those doors would start slamming again. I could hear them while I was changing the cartridges for the peep shows. But the peep show room had its own noises.

"There were a lot of stories about the Roxy's early years. During the thirties, gangsters would hide out there. Sometimes people were murdered. The Roxy had places most people didn't know about. One of them was a little hallway that came off the lobby and went all around the peep show area. There were six booths. From the hallway you could get into the back of each booth and its machine. I'd open up the back, change the cartridge, and take all the quarters. Built into the floor was a safe with a slot in its door. I'd drop the quarters into a zippered bank bag and go to the next booth. When I was done getting the quarters I dropped the bag through the slot in the safe.

"Sometimes I'd hear a gunshot down there, and a woman screaming. I'd peek out from behind the booth, and the place would be empty. Or there might be one person in one booth, yet there were voices in the room. The peep shows were like the theater. I didn't hear stuff every day. Just some days, and some weeks more than others."

I said that it seemed that some creepy things would happen just because of the nature of the audience.

"Oh, they did some things all right. Porno audiences can get mean. If something goes wrong, like the film breaks or you don't get a reel going fast enough, they get riled and start tearing up the place. But what I'm talking about is stuff they had nothing to do with."

I asked whether anyone ever bothered him in the booth.

"Funny you should ask that. One time I was rewinding the last reel after the last show. It's projectionist etiquette to leave the reel wound and threaded for the next guy before you leave. I was about done when I heard someone coming up the stairway. Ours was one of those metal L-shaped ones. He was coming up slowly, like he was drunk. The door into the booth from the stairs was closed. There's a gun in a drawer at the front of the booth. I got the gun out real quietly and waited. Whoever it was stopped at the top. I didn't hear anything. I watched the knob. It moved some like someone was turning it. But the door didn't open. I told whoever it was that nobody was allowed up there but me, and that they'd better leave. The knob stopped moving, but I couldn't hear anyone going back down. I told him again to leave. Nothing.

"I reached out and pulled open the door real fast-like, but there wasn't anybody there. I know that I had heard someone coming up the steps, and nothing had gone down. The footsteps had stopped at the top…but there wasn't anything there.

"That happened a couple more times that summer."

I asked whether he had any idea why some nights he never heard anything and other nights he did. Was it a full moon or something, or a particular day of the week? Was there any time that he could expect it to be a creepy night?

"No, I never knew what to expect.

"There was an old wino who worked the popcorn stand, but he never wanted to talk about any of that stuff. He probably wouldn't have noticed if the building was on fire. It was getting into August, and I was going back to school. Like I said, the owner was always real nice to me. I had been a good worker and hadn't stolen any quarters or anything. He took me out to dinner a few nights before my last night. It was that last night at work that was the noisiest.

"I had spent most of the day teaching the wino how to operate the projectors. He left about ten o'clock in the evening. Then it was just me and the audience. It was like all the sounds I'd ever heard had come back for an encore. The bathroom doors kept slamming, and the voices from the editing room were going on and on. Something kept coming up the stairway to the projection booth and stopping at the top. Between shows I heard screams and shouts and gunshots from someplace, but never any sirens. I was so glad when the last show was over…I was *scared*.

"When the last film finished and the first credits started to roll, I hit the dowser. A dowser works like a shutter and blocks the light from the carbon-arc lamphose, making the screen go dark. I turned on the house lights to empty the theater, left the projector running so the film would run out, and beat it to the peep show room, which had closed at nine o'clock. The peep show room was noisy too, but I still heard the *pop* sound when the film's tail leader hit the projector. The film's soundtrack had been playing before that. I worked fast because I kept hearing shots and screams and footsteps—some were in the peep show room, and some sounded like they were coming from the theater. When I was done with the booths and the quarters, I locked the peep show doors and went back to the theater.

"I was shaking. I didn't want to go back into the theater, but I had to clean the projectors, rewind the reels, get them in order, and thread the first two. I had to make things easy for the old wino—I didn't trust him. It was dark in the theater when I went in, and quiet. Real quiet. I had left the projector on, so there should have been a hum from it, and the noise of the film's end flopping against the projector as it went round and round. The bathroom doors didn't move or slam. It was way too quiet, but I don't think I could have gone in there if it had been noisy.

"I checked the house to make sure it was empty. Then I locked the theater doors and went up the metal stairs to the booth. I was glad I'd left the lights on up there. Then I opened the door."

I asked whether there were more noises.

"No, no noises. It was the projector. It had been turned off. Both projectors were all clean. All the reels had been rewound and were hanging on their pegs in the proper order. And the first two were already on the projectors, threaded and everything, ready to go."

I said that it was as if they had been throwing him a going-away party that night and then left him a present. They must have liked him.

"I guess so. I didn't spend much time thinking about it. I looked at the projectors for a minute...I couldn't believe it. Then all I could think of was getting out of there. I don't even remember leaving. All I remember is getting home that night, and then I got drunk. Real, real drunk."

Home Is Where
the Haunting Is:

Ghostly Houseguests

And Baby Makes Four

It had been a good morning in the clinic. All the children had been delightful. The families had shown up on time for their appointments, and I hadn't had to keep anyone waiting for more than a few minutes. The babies coming in for well-child checks were all cute but, from a medical standpoint, not very interesting. Dull days are the best kind. Then Carly showed up in her mother's arms. Carly beamed from her mother's lap, little suspecting that she was about to get impaled by a set of immunizations.

"How's she sleeping at night?" I asked.

"Oh, we're lucky. She sleeps through most of the night now. She is still in the room with us, till we get her into her own room."

"When will that be?" I asked.

"Well…" her mother's voice trailed off in embarrassment. "Our trailer is really nice. When we got it, no one had lived in it for years. But there's a problem with her room."

"Oh?" I asked.

"It sounds weird, but there are some strange things going on in there."

"Care to elaborate?" I inquired.

"We have her crib and a rocking chair in there already. But it's hard to go into the room and do anything because the dog won't let us in. He gets in the doorway and barks at something in there. Sometimes he stays down the hall and barks in the direction of the room. When we try to go in, he blocks our way."

"Why?"

"We don't know. There's nothing in there but the furniture. Once in a while we step in before he sees us, but as soon as we go in he runs in after us and stays in front of us like he's protecting us from something."

"What else happens?" I asked.

"Sometimes we hear soft footsteps in the room when no one is in there. We hear them in the rest of the trailer too, at night. I get scared at night when I'm alone. I don't like to be alone there. One time the dog was growling at the room, and I saw that the rocking chair had moved. It was next to the door that morning but later it was over next to the crib, leaning against it."

"What happens when you get into the room without the dog?" I asked.

"That's another problem. The room doesn't have an air conditioning unit in the window, but sometimes when I go in there it will be very cold, much colder than the outside or the other rooms. Then it will suddenly get hot, and a few minutes later cold again, just like turning something on and off."

"Nothing happens to your daughter?"

"No. She's a happy baby. But she's always with us."

"When will you let her stay in her room?" I asked.

"Not any time soon!" she laughed nervously. "We're going to have a priest bless the whole trailer first, and bless her room. We already have a bottle of holy water in every room. But it was strange: After we put a bottle in her room we found it later, tipped over with some of the water spilled out. Hers is the only room where that happened."

"That must have frightened you," I said.

"That's one of the reasons I'm afraid to be there alone at night. Sometimes we see shadows for no reason. One night I was alone, and before I went to bed I locked every window and door. I also locked the chain lock on the front door. I woke up a few hours later and checked the locks"—she shuddered at the memory—"and everything was unlocked. The chain lock had come undone, and the door was closed against the chain so that the end was hanging outside."

"So you made sure that no one could come in, but something may have gotten out?" I asked.

"Yes." And the dog had apparently remained asleep.

To Carly's displeasure, she still got her shots that day. I made a mental note to follow up later and see how things were going with her room.

When I heard this story, I could not help but think of the many skeptics who do not believe in ghosts or other unexplained phenomena. I know many people who don't want to talk about such things at all; they think that even talking about hauntings is evil. Others are visibly nervous when the subject comes up, which is understandable.

Let's say that you, the reader, are a skeptic and think that Carly's mother has an imagination that has run a little wild and that there are perfectly rational explanations for her family's experiences.

Would you let Carly sleep alone in her room?

Jennifer's Friend

When Jennifer's family visited the house on Tocques Place in St. Augustine and considered buying it, something or someone quickly got busy making friends. After the family moved in, Jennifer was in a bathroom when she noticed that the mirror, which was a little foggy, had writing on it. In backward cursive, it said, "Hi, Jennifer." She knew only a little cursive, and this was especially hard for her to read because it was backwards, but she did know her name.

Whereas Jennifer was not terribly bothered by her unseen friend, the family dogs apparently were. Both were large dogs who were well behaved, intelligent, not easily frightened, and capable of opening doors by themselves. After the family had bought and moved into the house, the dogs were left in Jennifer's room for a couple of hours while the family was away.

When the family returned, they found that the dogs had torn apart Jennifer's room and were still in it, though obviously upset. They had even had accidents on the carpet. No one could figure out why the dogs had not simply let themselves out of the room. Afterwards the dogs were left in other rooms, but the problem never occurred again.

Some things did happen again and again. The sound of a little boy crying for his mother was often heard. Once he was even seen sitting at the top of the stairs. Sometimes a little boy could be heard crying out for help from the front windowsill. On investigation, the boy was nowhere to be found.

No reason could be found for the frequent sounds of wind rushing through the attic. One of Jennifer's favorite teddy bears frequently disappeared. It was always found at the same spot near the top of her closet. Jennifer learned to climb up to that spot and retrieve the bear herself. Perhaps the wandering teddy bear was the work of a mischievous spirit.

Except for the incident with the dogs, Jennifer's family had no real trouble with their household spooks. Doors locked and unlocked by themselves, but no one was hurt or trapped. A woman with a long skirt on was sometimes seen walking through the house. One little girl who came to visit was behaving obnoxiously and not treating the children well. She left in a hurry after something unseen pushed her down.

Jennifer's aunt came to baby-sit while Jennifer's mother was away for a few days. Apparently she had not been told that she might find herself baby-sitting more than the three children she already knew. At night she had a vivid dream of a little boy (not Jennifer's brother) coming to her in her bedroom and begging her to come upstairs and see his room. Even though she did not recognize the boy, he was eager for her to follow him, and finally she rose from her bed and did so. On the way up the stairs she wondered who he was. As if he knew what she was thinking, he turned to her, smiled, and said helpfully, "I'm dead, you know."

She woke with a start. Both dogs were in her room; one was snapping at something above her that she could not see. She left as soon as Jennifer's mother returned, never to come back.

After some years, the house was sold again. Manifestations continued. After all the household goods had been taken out, the family returned to clean the house. Red liquid, looking like blood, was oozing from a banister. The mother thought this was a sign that the ghosts were sad about their leaving. Amazingly, the family had gotten so used to the ghosts that they calmly finished cleaning before leaving.

Eventually the ghosts left as well. The next owners were not as tolerant as Jennifer's family had been and asked a priest to bless the house. The manifestations then stopped. As far as we know, Jennifer's family never again encountered ghosts, much to the relief of certain aunts and dogs.

The Quietest Neighbors

Some neighborhoods are more crowded than others. This can be due to zoning, the type of houses, or presence of apartment complexes and condominiums. Or cemeteries, as the case is in Tallahassee. Oakland Cemetery is the focus of a few rumors. Yet cemeteries tend to be unnerving places in themselves; we stereotype them as being creepy places to be at night. We don't often consider their effect on the neighborhoods around them.

Happily, Oakland Cemetery does not seem to represent the wrong side of the tracks. Such was the experience of a nurse while she was attending Florida State University. She lived with her pet cat and a roommate in an apartment near Oakland Cemetery. One chilly spring day she was curled up sleeping in her bed when she was awakened by footsteps in her apartment. There were voices in the living room. She thought her roommate had come home.

Tallahassee's Oakland Cemetery
Photograph by Crystal Sirmans

Looking up from her bed, she was rudely surprised to see a young man in her bedroom. He wore a red flannel work shirt with blue checks. His hair was a dirty blond color.

She certainly minded his being there uninvited, but her cat didn't mind a bit. The man was petting the cat, and the cat was savoring every minute. Before the nurse could say anything, her visitor turned and walked toward the door. She called her roommate's name twice but there was no sound save footsteps. Then he was gone, before he even reached the door.

Pulling open her door, she could hear footsteps, but no one could be seen. A quick check of the apartment showed nothing but locked doors and windows. The voices and the footsteps were gone by then. What remains is her certainty that she saw and heard a ghost. As for the voices in the living room, she had no explanation.

Had it been Oakland Cemetery's welcome wagon?

Bill

"My husband doesn't believe in ghosts or anything like that, so he thinks I'm being silly," she told me. "I hope he's right. I hope that it's just my imagination."

If it wasn't just her imagination, Jenny and her husband had better take out some good insurance and make friends with the local police and firefighters. The "it" she spoke of is a series of experiences that began in New York.

"There was a house where some of my friends lived where strange things would happen. They thought it was because of a ghost, and they named him Bill. Sometimes the lights would go on and off for no reason. We would be the only ones in the house and no one was near a switch."

Could it have been power problems? She didn't think so. There were other appliances in the house that worked just fine. I thought that perhaps a bad fuse to the lighting system might do it. But then she went on.

"The strangest thing was the appliances. Things like a dishwasher or a radio would turn on all by themselves. Of course a radio might have a timer, but not a vacuum cleaner or anything."

Any electric appliance could be plugged into a timer that could be plugged into a wall. But she had seen no timers. Television sets, other radios, anything electrical was fair game for Bill. Things in the house would be found in places other than where they had been left.

Had she seen any of these things happen herself? Why was she worried now?

"Oh yes—lots. My friends said it happened more often when I was around. I never saw anything move but I was there when things turned on and off by themselves. I saw the lights flickering sometimes. That's one of the things that bothers me now—that it seemed to have something to do with my being around.

"One day my friend got scratched by Bill. I guess she had done something he didn't like. She was getting dressed and something scratched her hard down her back. She had three scratch marks down her back, like claw marks. After that, they decided to get rid of Bill. They talked to a priest and made an appointment for him to come over and do a blessing or an exorcism."

I asked her if it worked.

"They never got a chance. The day before the priest was supposed to come over, the house burned down. It was weird. They couldn't find a cause of the fire. They couldn't even figure out where it started. It was like the entire house started burning at once. There was nothing left."

I asked what happened then.

"Later I got married. My husband's job made us travel to different places before we finally settled down here. We go back to New York where the house used to stand to visit sometimes, but we haven't heard of any more of Bill." She grinned nervously. "But I'm a little scared now because of our radio. My husband has our stereo and TV and radio all wired together so that they use the same speakers. The radio comes on by itself, every twelve hours for a few days. My husband says that it's the timer acting up. But nothing else comes on and it's all connected together. He thinks I'm imagining things. He doesn't believe in ghosts or anything like that. Especially he does not believe that Bill might have followed me here."

I told her that I just hoped he was right.

Charlotte

Halloween was just past. A group of neighbors and I were relaxing around a bonfire in Lakeland, destroying marshmallows, burning food, and acquiring first-degree burns. We are men, I thought, and this is how we cook: put the food near a heat source (the more life threatening the better) and then retrieve it before it turns to ashes. If it is charred, it is good. To cook any other way, we would have to ask for directions. We don't ask for directions.

I marveled at the taste of molten marshmallow. Until I could feel my tongue again, I decided to keep quiet and listen to the others.

"The new family's not saying anything about Charlotte."

"Have you met them?"

"No, but someone I know has. He asked about Charlotte. They said they hadn't seen or heard anything. But they were real quiet. They didn't seem to want to talk about her."

My eyes opened wide and I shrugged my shoulders, trying to look quizzical. My mouth was full of something that had been put into a bun and handed to me. At last someone explained:

"There's a house near here that had a ghost. That's what the family said that lived there, and the family before them. They weren't afraid of her or anything. The only reason the last family moved was because they were military and got transferred."

"How did they know she was there?" I asked.

"They would hear footsteps in a hall or a room when nobody was there. Sometimes things got moved without anyone knowing who had done it. She never caused any trouble. I guess she liked the people who lived there. They took good care of the place. What was strange was when they decided to move and had the real estate agent come over."

"What happened?" I was becoming interested.

"They told the agent about Charlotte, and she just laughed. She didn't think it would be a good idea to advertise a haunted house. She didn't say anything bad about Charlotte. But when she had finished looking around the house and was ready to leave, she couldn't find her car keys. They looked all over the house, but the keys were gone. Finally they found them on a stand outside next to the front door. She had no idea how they had gotten there out of her purse."

I frowned. "Maybe she was just absent-minded, being busy looking at the house."

"Not the second time, or the third. Three of the times she came to the house, her keys disappeared right out of her purse and were found outside, near the front door."

"But the house got sold?" I asked. "Where is it? I'd like to meet the owners if possible, and ask them about Charlotte."

"They sure don't seem to want to talk about her."

"Maybe someday, then. But I'll keep a good tight grip on my keys."

The Scene of the Crime

The house in Clermont was and still is the scene of the only unsolved murder in the county. In 1975, its owner, dressed in blue jeans and a denim shirt, rushed out to the driveway to put out a small fire that had started in his truck. He was successful, but he never left the driveway. A shotgun at close range had taken care of that. Had he gotten back to the house, he would have found the phone lines cut. The fire was almost certainly a lure to an ambush. There was no known motive, no suspect, no solution, and no closure.

Later a TV crew from *Unsolved Mysteries* was invited to film there and publicize the case. However, instead of helping find the murderer, they found the victim.

He has been seen many times, the man in denim. He has been photographed. He has even materialized in front of people in the house. When seen, there is also a sensation of cold and an acrid smell described as a mixture of ammonia, sulfur, and a smelly sock. When he vanishes, a cold rush of wind is felt.

One visitor saw him in a second-story hallway—upon rushing back down the hall after telling others, he saw a host of angels marching through the same hallway. Other visitors have found music boxes playing by themselves.

Is the ghost trying to say that he will come and go as he pleases? Doorknobs have turned by themselves, an indoor rocker has rocked by itself, and outside, a swing careens wildly back and forth on a calm day, demanding to be noticed. Some people think that the spirit intends to stay at the house till the murder is solved and that he does not want to be forgotten. The police have kept the case open, but it is Clermont's only unsolved murder.

The ghost has never appeared to his widow. She lives nearby. She visited the house once after the new owners moved in, but her late husband didn't show himself. He has been known to show up when practically dared to do so. One guest at a dinner party kept cracking jokes about the spirit till an apparition actually materialized in front of everyone.

The house where the murder happened, near downtown Clermont, gets a lot of children on Halloween and gawkers at other times. Strange things still happen, but not everything can be blamed on the ghost. One day, while one of the owners was preparing dinner in the kitchen, the figure of a woman appeared in the kitchen with her. Astonished, the owner realized that the woman was as real as she was and not a ghost.

"Oh, I just couldn't leave Florida without seeing the haunted house," the stranger smiled, fully aware that she was on private property. Apparently she felt that since ghosts aren't known to be subject to trespassing laws, those who were interested in ghosts shouldn't be either.

Fordham House

One of the largest wedding gifts ever given in Pensacola is the Fordham House. It was given to Laura Moreno by her father for her wedding to Dr. William Fordham in 1875. As the years went by, eventually the house was occupied by Ernestine Fordham Nathan. She died in the back room of the house.

Since Ernestine's death, life in the house has gotten more interesting. The house was restored and opened for rental parties in 1986. Evanescent shadows were seen in large mirrors. Footsteps were heard coming down an empty hallway. Sometimes petticoats were heard rustling.

The owners decided that the house was haunted but by a friendly and benign ghost. They must have been tolerant people. Once they locked a door with a deadbolt, and it opened by itself later. The floor where some of Ernestine's furniture had sat will not take a stain. One night some jewelry belonging to one of the owners vanished; it was found the next day in Ernestine's back room. All of the clasps had been fastened. All could be unfastened except one. It was secured permanently.

There was also a day during the restoration of the house when tools went flying across a room for no discernible reason. The work of a friendly ghost? Or maybe the work of an all-too-human, charmingly klutzy, likes-to-be-noticed ghost? You decide. Remember that Ernestine may still have feelings. If you're ever in the area of the Fordham House and have an opinion about Ernestine, the courteous thing to do is to feel free to keep it to yourself.

A Visit with Grampa

The children live near Fort Meade, out amid the citrus groves in a quiet, rural lifestyle. None are yet old enough to go to elementary school. Like Sara herself, they see Sara's grandfather sometimes. They know that Grampa died several years ago. Their parents have told them so.

"I think that children see things that we don't," Sara's mother, Claire, told me. "Sara got past the people who were supposed to be watching her during the viewing after her grampa died. She saw him in the casket. She knows that he's in heaven. But every now and then she comes in and says that she has seen him."

"Oh?" I replied. "For how long?"

"Since after he died. She's not frightened or anything. It's not just her. Other children who live near us have seen their uncle, who died a little while ago…even ones who have never seen their uncle alive. They all like him."

"How does anybody know who these men are?" I asked.

"Sara knows her grandfather because she remembers him. We've asked the others what the man they see looks like, and they all describe the same person. No adult ever sees him, even if he has been in the yard."

I was doubtful. "These are small children. What kind of detailed description could they give?"

"They tell us what he is wearing. The clothes they tell us about are clothes we know he used to wear."

"Are there pictures of him around the house that they might have seen? Perhaps wearing the clothes they describe?"

"No. That's one of the strange things. How could they know what he liked to wear?"

"What is Grampa doing when Sara sees him? Or the other man?" I asked.

"Sara and the other children say that each one smiles and watches them. Sometimes they tell the kids things."

I was intrigued. "Such as?"

"Sara says that Grampa has told her that he is very happy. He also says that he is watching over her, even when she can't see him. One time Sara came in and said, 'Grampa says that he's got a new body.' I went out to look, but of course I couldn't see anyone outside. It's like he visits us but only shows himself to the children. Or maybe it's only children who can see him. They're not afraid of him at all. I'm glad of that. Like I said, I think that children can see things that we grownups can't. I believe that Sara is seeing my father."

Maybe we lose something as we get older. Or is it that we gain something? I'm not sure. Next time I see Sara, I'll ask her to ask Grampa about it.

The Electronic Ghost

Is it possible for a home security system to detect a ghost? This may have happened in a home in Pensacola recently. A security system was in place while this house was between owners. Before the buyers moved in, the company had a problem with the alarm going off frequently, yet no person or any signs of attempted entry were found. That is, till one of the new owners happened to come in just as the alarm was going off yet again. She glanced about the obviously empty house and called the alarm company to report that there were no intruders other than herself.

Everything seemed fine till the company's monitors showed that a motion sensor had activated in a room on the far side of the house. They immediately told her, but she could see no one. One by one, motion sensors activated—the company could see that something or someone was moving in her direction. The owner was unconcerned. She could see nothing coming toward the room in which she stood.

Whatever it was, it almost reached her. By now the operator was nearly in a frenzy—she begged the owner to get out of the house immediately. The woman did so safely.

Can a motion sensor detect a ghost? There is a theory that ghosts are forms of electromagnetic energy. If a ghost is invisible, then it's unlikely that a motion sensor could detect one, unless a ghost's "body" or essence blocks infrared light, which motion sensors use to detect movement. Another way a motion sensor could be tripped is if magnetic energy caused a current to flow within the sensor. A moving magnetic field creates electrical current, and a sensor uses relatively little current to operate. As a test, I tried moving a strong magnet next to a motion sensor in my house. Nothing happened.

Another potential flaw in the story is the use of the telephone. Home security systems will "capture" the phone line forty seconds after activation. No matter who is trying to tie up the phone, the system will take over and transmit its message. Therefore it would be impossible for the system to be activated and for the owner to talk on the phone for more than forty seconds.

Unless, of course, the owner was using a cellular phone.

Party!

It was a dark and stormy night. Florida has had its share of those, but this was not just another such night in Florida. It was a dark and stormy night in Lloyd, which sits on Interstate 10 just east of Tallahassee. It wasn't just another night in Lloyd either. It was a night at Grandma's old, old farmhouse—the location of the longest-running party in Florida.

Thirteen-year-old Bobbie Jo was spending the night with her friend Kaylee in the mobile home next to the old farmhouse where Kaylee's grandmother lived. Bobbie Jo wasn't used to the sounds of wind and rain on the outside of a mobile home. She lay awake while Kaylee slept. The trailer shook from the wind.

Over the sound of the rain she heard the car. It certainly wasn't the wind whining out there. This car was a clunker and sounded like one of those that racked up more miles being towed or pushed than moving under its own power. The headlight beams reflected from the trees and raindrops as the car passed by.

Whoever was in the car was oblivious to the storm. Four car doors opened and shut. She heard the laughter of people close to her own age, as well as the barking of a dog that seemed to be playing with them. The front door of the farmhouse kept screeching open and slamming shut as people traipsed in and out. Despite the wind and rain, the front porch swing's chains were clinking from use. People were talking and enjoying themselves despite the miserable weather.

Wondering what kind of family members Kaylee had not told her about, Bobbie Jo looked out the window. No car. No people. No dog. A closed door on a dark house. But the sounds of a great party could still be heard.

She woke Kaylee, who told her, "It's ghosts. Everybody's heard them. Go back to sleep."

The following morning Bobbie Jo asked Kaylee's sister about the party, only to find out that she had had similar experiences, except that she had never seen the car lights.

No one has identified who the partygoers are. Whoever they are, they have kept the festivities going for years. There is no record of any party in Lloyd that ended in tragedy for all concerned. All we know is that in the little town of Lloyd, there are some entities who really know how to have a good time.

Higgins' Haunted Home

On a bright and sunny day I drove through wide expanses of land that had been stripped of all vegetation in preparation for construction. Along the road past the barren landscape were orange groves typical of central Florida. Just inside the orange groves was a neighborhood of well-tended, middle-class homes. I cruised the streets till I found the address I had been given.

The house was brightly colored, sitting in a yard even better kept than those of the neighbors. There was nothing sinister about it from its appearance. Nearby, the local children played without a care. They were scrambling over some playground equipment. One girl was the smallest, the most fragile looking, and the loudest. She was clearly the one in charge.

Years ago, the one-story, three-bedroom concrete block house in Lake Wales seemed just right for the Higgins family. It wasn't till after Jim and Betty Higgins and their son, Lance, moved in that they discovered the home's other residents — the ones who paid no rent.

Lance was the first to meet one of them. He looked up to see a girl in the doorway of his bedroom. As he spoke to her, she turned and disappeared down the hallway. He hurriedly checked one room after another and found them all empty save for the ones that were locked, and all of them were locked from the inside.

Soon the living residents of the house were comparing notes on their sightings. A houseguest claimed that there were ghosts in the house. Betty Higgins saw "something in white" disappear into the living room as she stood in the kitchen. Smoky apparitions were seen, usually accompanied by an odor of sulfur. Mary Beth, who married Lance and moved into the house, had been there only three nights before running from their bedroom, screaming about a ghost.

The phenomena increased in variety. Betty got her first good look at the spirit of a man who was wearing a plaid shirt. More than just people and ghosts were moving about — covers that had been kicked off a bed were found neatly folded. Papers that had blown off a dresser reappeared on top of the dresser in a tidy stack. So far the spirits seemed benign and even helpful, except for the sulfurous odor.

The Higginses were understandably curious as to why so many supernatural events were going on in their rented home. They tried using a Ouija board but didn't learn anything — until later.

Only a block away, the Luthers also had a pair of uninvited but harmless guests who were thought to be responsible for occasional unexplained thumping in the house. Once Mrs. Luther saw a pair of translucent figures. Occasionally her husband would feel something rubbing his back lightly. The Luthers and their housemates got along fine.

In contrast, the Higgins home was getting to be more and more unnerving. Walls began to vibrate. More objects moved by themselves. Whispering was heard. Cold spots and hot spots appeared and vanished for no explainable reason. No one knew from moment to moment what would be found on the other side of any door. Despite the reports he was getting from the rest of the household, Jim declined to believe that anything supernatural was happening.

It was around that time that Mary Beth Higgins was suddenly and briefly possessed. With astounding strength for her 105-pound frame, she attacked and pinned her 260-pound husband to a bed. He was unable to break free of her grip until he was able to hit her against a wall hard enough to leave bruises on her back. When she was herself again, she remembered or believed nothing until the bruises were pointed out.

That's when Jim became a believer. "If there's a possession taking place, you can't ignore it."

Subsequently, both Jim and Betty felt something trying to possess them as well. They successfully resisted but had problems with unexplained chills and headaches afterwards. Home was for safety and family was for security, but their home and family were less safe and secure each day. No one knew when the next possession or threat would come, or whether the others would be asleep and helpless when it happened. No one knew if it would happen to a person who was near a butcher knife. And both Betty and Mary Beth knew their husbands, who towered over them both, would need no weapons in their hands if they suddenly turned from protective husbands into...what?

It was time to get some help.

The elder Higginses went to a woman who was a spiritualist and gave them a formula to rid the house of ghosts, as well as some prayers to help the dead on their way. She was also greatly concerned about the Ouija board. She told them they were dangerous for amateurs to use and that Ouija boards were known to attract entities from the wrong side of the spiritual tracks who could make things unpleasant indeed.

Lance and Mary Beth Higgins went to a local numerologist who was also a hypnotist/healer. He visited the house and evaluated it for intersections of "lines of negative force," which were thought to be portals for unwelcome spirits. Such an intersection was found at one bedroom doorway. He performed a cleansing ceremony using incense, candles placed at specific locations, prayers, and a crystal. The elder Higginses did as their spiritualist consultant had advised as well.

Afterwards there seemed to be a decrease in spirit activity. The family tried to cope through a shared sense of humor. "Ghostbusters" T-shirts were a household fashion, and the doormat read "Boo." A yellow triangular sign stood in a hallway reading "Yield to Ghosts." It was not enough. The younger Higginses moved out, and the older ones began to look elsewhere for another place to rent. In the meantime, a local historian commented that the neighborhood was close to a former cemetery from which the bodies had been moved to another location. Jim Higgins felt that perhaps some of the spirits had stayed behind.

That explanation may have sufficed, but for the media coverage of all that had gone on. A man who had lived next door and then moved before the Higginses moved into the house was particularly struck by Betty's accounts of a ghost with a plaid shirt. He visited them and asked Betty to describe what she saw more fully, for his deceased father had always worn a plaid shirt. She had no trouble remembering, for she had just awakened very recently to see a man with a plaid shirt walking through their bedroom and exiting through a solid wall. Betty's description matched that of the neighbor's late father, whom Betty had never met. And the father had not been buried in the nearby cemetery.

Some thing seemed determined to keep the family from making the house a home. The county sheriff's records show that police were called a number of times to go to that location during the time that the Higginses lived there, but no reasons for the calls show up in the reports. There are no reports of what was found at the house either. Perhaps the investigating officers decided to leave well enough alone. After all, what could they take into custody?

The Gray House of Pensacola

When an unsuspecting family bought the Gray House in Pensacola, they had no idea that the house had a built-in security system, one that charged no fees and required no hardware.

A presence was noticed in the house soon after the family moved in. Footsteps were heard on the front staircase when no one was there; in fact, the entire family was listening to them while seated around the dinner table. A musky smell was noted once without obvious origin. A roomer once heard someone going about banging doors downstairs while the house was otherwise empty. One owner found herself speaking aloud, answering questions, though she was alone.

Windows and doors were found to have opened by themselves. Objects were found in places other than where they were left. Lights flickered for no reason, and sets of objects were found rearranged. An empty rocking chair was observed once, rocking in time to some music that was playing. Many of the events were of a playful nature, and in fact, sounds of children playing were heard when the family's own children were all out of the house.

Events then became more serious but not malevolent. A friend's dog trembled and moaned in the back hallway till taken home. A worker left a can of kerosene in a hallway; the following morning, the can had mysteriously moved outside the house. A pack of cigarettes was left on a nightstand one night. The next day, each of the cigarettes was found to have tiny holes punched in it. Candles and matches were found broken. A security alarm kept going off for no reason.

A séance was held, as well as a session with a Ouija board. The name of Thomas Moristo came repeatedly. Investigation showed that a Moristo had never owned the house, but a Thomas Moristo may have once owned the tract of land behind the house. In addition, it was found that Moristo was a sea captain who had once come home to his sweetheart to find her gone and the house partially burned.

There was still the problem of the security alarm going off. It was as if the ghost had fears that were being expressed through the alarms. Finally the exasperated alarm company resorted to sending a representative to the house to speak aloud to the ghost. He asked the spirit to stop setting off the alarms unless there was a good reason; otherwise the house would be endangered because either the system would have to be removed or no one would answer a real alarm because of all the false ones.

There hasn't been a false alarm since. Things left overnight in one place still show up in another place the next morning, and in the nighttime the sound of a chair rolling across the upstairs floor can be heard. At least, however, the earthly and the supernatural guardians of the Gray House have learned to work together.

Close Encounters
of the Past Kind:
Historical Haunts

There Goes the Neighborhood

Just outside the old city gates of St. Augustine on its north end is the Huguenot Cemetery. In this place of the dead, some are more dead than others. Judge Stickney's restless spirit, often seen wandering through the cemetery at night, has a legitimate set of grievances, but there is no earthly judge for him to take them to.

The honorable judge, then a widower, came to St. Augustine with his children just after the Civil War. Being from Massachusetts, there was naturally some talk of his being yet another carpetbagger. There is no record of how he felt about those charges. There are plenty of records of what he did about them: He lived a life of integrity in St. Augustine as a district and state attorney. He became a prominent and respected citizen in what he clearly felt was his new home.

St. Augustine's Huguenot Cemetery

Sadly, his children were orphaned when the judge died of typhoid fever on a business trip to Washington, D.C. He had indicated that he wished to be buried in St. Augustine. His body was brought back and interred in Huguenot Cemetery in 1882, to be at rest with his fellow citizens.

The rest of Judge Stickney's story began innocently enough after his death. His children were adopted by a family friend, Judge Long, who brought them up in Washington, D.C., as his own—so much so that when Judge Long died in 1903, the Stickney offspring requested that their father's body be exhumed and brought to Washington, to be buried beside that of Judge Long.

Judge Stickney's casket was accordingly dug up and opened. A crowd of onlookers gathered at the rare spectacle, pressing ever closer to the open casket. When the worker opened the lid, it was clear that the remains were well preserved and definitely those of the judge. Two of the onlookers had been drinking heavily. As the worker dispersed the crowd, he looked back and was aghast to see the judge's bones being rummaged through by the two drunks. They got away with all the judge's gold teeth. What remained in the casket was carefully rearranged by a mortician and closed up securely.

After this indignity, the judge was reburied in Washington, D.C. Despite being buried in that city next to his longtime friend, his spirit is seen not in Washington but in St. Augustine. The impression of the numerous people who have seen him is that he is looking for something. Perhaps it is his lost teeth, which may have been hocked to finance more drunken escapades. Perhaps it is his body, taken against his request from the city he called home. Or perhaps it is just his lost dignity.

The insults weren't over yet. If he kept up on such things, he would know that the St. Augustine cemetery, where his spirit had remained, was now also the final resting place of the widow of the Casablanca Inn, the notorious accomplice of rumrunners in the 1920s (See chapter 8.). However, by the time she was placed there, he didn't have a grave to spin in.

But that is another story.

Old Leon County Jail

Theories abound about ghosts and how they come about. A popular one is that they are associated with places where there has been great emotional upheaval and stress. A Floridian spin on this idea is that ghosts are associated with hidden pirate treasure. The pirates seem to feel that if they can't take it with them, then they'll make sure that nobody else takes it anywhere. Hidden or stored treasure brings out all sorts of weirdness in people, even the dead.

In Tallahassee, the site of the old Leon County Jail (closed in the 1960s) is said to have been a storage place for Spanish treasure. There is little question that emotional stress and upheaval occurred there. A fellow being held overnight for a relatively minor infraction might find himself with a cellmate or two who were in for far more violent and despicable crimes, and no one knew for certain whether the other had truly repented of his sins. Brutal people were caged there together. Some killed themselves. Some killed others. One report says that during renovations about thirty years ago, two skeletons were found in a small compartment behind a wall.

One worker in the building paused on the way up some stairs and felt someone tap his shoulder. No one was there when he turned around. Others have had something or someone unseen brush past them or push them while on the stairs.

One man was working late one night, looking forward to a quiet evening of productivity. He didn't get it. Something was banging the other side of the wall behind him with what sounded like a sledgehammer. The loud pounding went on for hours till he thought the wall would crumble. The next morning he looked at the other side of the wall to see how much damage had been done. Not a mark was on it. There wasn't supposed to be any remodeling work at that time either. The hammering has never been explained.

The same person was working late another night when he heard some unusual noises. It was half past two in the morning and no one else was supposed to be in the building. As he went around a corner to find their cause, he saw a cell door swing open by itself, pause momentarily, then close again. There might have been air circulation from the air conditioning system, but not anything sufficient to open a mass of steel bars that weighed over a hundred pounds. That would have required winds of hurricane velocity, and there are no records of stray hurricanes having been detained in the Leon County Jail.

Naturally, the circulating stories attracted interest. A psychic tried to hold a séance at the former jail. Supposedly, five of the participants were in contact with spirits. The spirits proved to be so malevolent that the séance was broken off. Now even the psychics seem to shun investigations of the old jail.

Certainly the former inmates would want to forget that the jail ever existed. Those who have never been there might want to follow their example.

Old Bradford House

I *got great days ahead of me, when my children grow up. Silk dress-es, fur coats, and diamond rings.* —Arizona Donnie Barker, to her neighbors.

For all the trouble the dead woman in Florida was going to cause him, he may as well have shot her himself and draped her body across his desk, behind the nameplate that identified him as J. Edgar Hoover. Only one bullet had found and killed her. The public might have a problem with the fact that nearly fifteen hundred more had been fired at her house by his men.

It was 1935. Motherhood was still respected. Technically this meant that although she was dead, he and she were still at war. Ever mindful of the public relations aspect of his position, Mr. Hoover began a hatchet job on Ma Barker's reputation. It was not his job to care if Ma Barker would resist.

So Mr. Hoover and a cooperative press created two Ma Barkers: a cunning, ruthless, cigar-smoking crime lord who had raised her sons to steal, and a negligent mother who had not cared enough to intervene when her sons began going wrong.

The sons of "Bloody Mama" were the core of a gang that rampaged through the Midwest from 1931 to 1935. In their wake were murders, kidnappings, jailbreaks, mail robberies, burglaries, daring escapes, and the looting of trains and banks. Ma never participated in any of these crimes, and there is almost no basis for her reputation as a criminal mastermind. A gang member later commented that Ma Barker "couldn't plan a breakfast." When a job was being plotted in her home, she preferred to stay in another room, listening to hillbilly music or comedy acts on the radio.

The love of hillbilly music came from Ma Barker's roots. She was born Arizona Donnie Clark in the Ozarks, near Springfield, Missouri. At age fourteen she married George Barker, who was eighteen years older than she. Next year their first son Herman was born. Within ten years they had three more sons: Lloyd, Arthur ("Dock"), and Frederick.

The family was poor, and this was blamed largely on George, who was described as shiftless. George's real problem may have been too many shifts. He was a worker in the local lead and zinc mines. Lead does nothing to the human body except poison it, causing anemia and brain damage, among other problems. Lead workers did not have enough protection while working. Each day that they showed up for work they went home a little sicker. The lead dust on their clothing poisoned some of the people at home, too. As the years went on and Barkers kept dying, it was supposedly shiftless George who would pay to send for the bodies and have them properly buried in the family cemetery.

The boys, who were spending their idle time away from home and getting into what trouble they could find, weren't around the household as much as their parents. The parents brought the toxic dust home on their clothing and handled the dust by washing those clothes. As George grew less and less functional, he deferred all but the simplest tasks to his wife, who had picked up the nickname of Kate. Those who complained of the boys' rowdiness and petty thievery were referred to Kate. Those who went to Kate were called liars and driven off. Unable to see any wrong in her sons, Bloody Mama would have been more appropriately called Blind Mama.

Even as her sons compiled arrest records and moved her from place to place as they stayed ahead of the law, Ma Barker maintained that her children were good people who had been forced into lives of crime by the groundless persecution of the law. She did like the money that came in, whether handed to her by one of her sons' fleeing accomplices or sent to her from jail.

"Ma didn't like female competition. She wanted to be the only woman who counted with her boys," said Alvin Karpis, a leader within the gang. Ma knew that floozies and hussies could take her sons from her and bring back the hard times of 1928, when all the boys were in jail except for Herman, who had committed suicide as the police closed in on him for yet another robbery and murder. Kate Barker left George and acquired a boyfriend. George moved back to Missouri. He spent his remaining years operating a filling station. He filled cars with gasoline and the local cemetery with Barker bodies.

With sons Dock, Lloyd, and Fred remaining, Ma kept moving over the subsequent years, from Missouri to Minnesota to Reno, and so on. Soon it was just Dock and Fred, for Lloyd was languishing in Leavenworth prison. Ma was always hospitable to her sons' business associates, including "Machine Gun" Kelly.

In 1934 the Justice Department learned through informers that some of the people they were looking for were in the Barker gang, who traveled with an old woman and who were holed up in an apartment in Chicago. In January of 1935 the apartment was located and surrounded. Three of the occupants surrendered peacefully. A fourth, Russell Gibson, was wearing a bulletproof vest and tried to shoot his way out with a .32 automatic and a Browning automatic rifle. The vest did not work as well as intended—a .351 slug from the FBI went through the vest's front and did a lethal amount of damage before flattening against the inside back of the vest. (At least the vest had stopped the bullet from going out.) Gibson died soon afterward, cursing all law enforcement officials but strangely silent concerning the manufacturers of bulletproof vests.

Dock Barker was captured the same night at another apartment. Ma and Fred Barker had escaped by going on ahead to their next location. Inside Dock's apartment, officials found a map of Florida with the Ocala region circled.

The Barkers' presence in the area of Oklawaha and Lake Weir did not contribute anything to crime in the area. They lived quietly. Fred spent much time hunting a well-known huge alligator named "Old Joe." Fred had not yet gone out on the early morning that Federal agents quietly crept up to the house.

Nowadays tall hedges that block a gawker's view from the road surround the privately owned house. One would have to be inside to hear the phantom footsteps from the empty stairway, or in the upstairs bedroom where the apparition of a woman appears, combing her dark hair. The sounds of a card game from the empty parlor suggest a quiet family spending a morning together at home.

Then came a knock on the door. Sixty-three-year-old Ma Barker answered. Son Fred stepped from behind her with a machine gun and opened fire on the government agents. The next four to five hours were the longest gunfight in the history of the Justice Department. The shooting was almost continuous from both sides. The government agents, for their part, fired over fifteen hundred rounds at the house. Then those within stopped shooting.

After an hour of silence from the house, the Barkers' handyman was sent in to assess the situation. He had reason to be nervous. There were over thirty-five hundred holes in the house, caused by bullets from both sides. Willie Woodberry stepped onto the porch and called out, "It's me, Ma—don't shoot!"

Nobody shot. One man was dead on the stairs. Fred was dead upstairs with fourteen bullets in him. Ma lay nearby, with one bullet hole in her. A machine gun lay between them.

No crimes were being planned in the household where the Justice Department officials (who would later form the FBI) shot Ma Barker to death, probably not intending to do so. Rifles, pistols, cash, and plenty of ammunition were found in the house as well. None of these things show up as apparitions now. It is as if the spirit of Ma Barker does not remember them or want anyone else to remember her that way.

The cash amounted to over fourteen thousand dollars. A check of the serial numbers of the bills proved it was not ransom money. George asked for and got the money. He used part of it to bring Fred and Kate Barker to the family plot in Missouri, after their bodies had mummified in Ocala's mortuary for a few months.

Lloyd was eventually paroled from Leavenworth. He went straight. While Lloyd was going straight, his wife was going insane. One day she picked up a shotgun and put an end to his law-abiding life.

Of the other three brothers, only Dock Barker was still alive, in Alcatraz. He shed no more light on what kind of person his mother truly was. His last words were during an unsuccessful escape attempt—"I'm all shot to hell!"

The ghosts of the house in Oklawaha are not those of Bloody Mama or Don't-Care Mama. Both were creations of the Justice Department for the benefit of a public that might get up in arms over Kate Barker's death. Other gangsters' mothers were still alive and had been given only short jail terms for harboring their fugitive children. As for Mrs. Barker, she may still be holed up in the house, acting the way she wants herself and her family to be remembered. J. Edgar Hoover is dead, but she may be going on, protesting his impostor ghosts of Ma Barker.

See Rollie Run

Rollie Johnson watched as darkness fell. Tonight was going to be a special night but not the kind he looked forward to. The nights of full moons were enough of a nuisance. This night, Halloween night, was always the worst one of the year. He wished that he could pluck the last night of October from the calendar as easily as he could a diseased orange from Mr. Gamble's grove. Then he would fling it into Spruce Creek and watch it plop beneath the green water. He would never see it again. He would never miss it, either. There were plenty of healthier oranges on the trees and plenty of more respectable nights in the year.

Late in December, Mr. Gamble would come from Cincinnati to stay for a few months. He had done so for a few years already and would continue to do so for almost seventy years. Rollie Johnson was entrusted with the care of Gamble Place all year, and so he lived there alone from sometime in March till late December. He did not know if Mr. Gamble was trusting him or punishing him by expecting him to be there on Halloween.

On the night before November, Rollie Johnson was always alone—till the critters got loose.

He checked the citrus-packing barn, retrieving and lighting his lantern. Then he inspected Mr. Gamble's bungalow. It was part hunting lodge and part winter retreat as well. Everything was in order. He locked the doors. The critters had never gotten into the bungalow and trashed it since it had been built in 1907. For that he was grateful.

He kept the lantern covered. He was bigger than anything he would be chasing that night, but that meant they could hide in small, dark places he could not get to easily. It was best to sneak up on them or to catch one as it scampered by.

In his peripheral vision, he glimpsed a small, dark shape vanishing into the night. A second one giggled and approached him, springing to one side as Rollie gave chase. He recognized the gnome as they both crashed through the brush. Years of experience had prepared Rollie for what happened next: another gnome stepped out from behind a small azalea bush and tried to distract him. It was one of the fat ones, just slow enough to be surprised and caught as Rollie leaped and cleared the bush, reaching out with his free hand. Rollie gripped the gnome's shoulder. Dropping the lantern, he pinned the critter's other arm to its side. It turned out to be an unnecessary move; his catch was already turning to stone.

Rollie carried the stone statue back to where it had come from. He replaced it in its spot along a walkway. There were a number of other empty spots along that and other walkways. It was going to be a long night. Whatever he did not catch and return to its place or whatever did not come back by itself would have to be searched for and found in the weeks before Mr. Gamble's yacht came up the Spruce, bearing Mr. Gamble and his entourage.

The Gambles were not to blame for the Halloween problems. James Gamble, the oldest son of the man who had formed the famous partnership with Mr. Proctor, was a good employer and friend. Whatever family member had brought the stone figures to be placed along the walkways had had no idea that they might sometimes come to life. It was Rollie Johnson's fate to deal with the gleeful and elusive figures dashing throughout Gamble Place, and no one's fault.

Rollie took a break and went back to his own quarters for the bottle that would help him get through the night. He had taken the precaution of wearing his sturdiest boots. No one was around to object if he took his frustrations out on the one part of the 150-acre

Gnome with bucket
Courtesy of Daytona Museum of Arts and Sciences

plantation that he hated unceasingly. No matter what came to life and ran off, the magnolia tree would squat smugly right where it had been for over two hundred years. Rollie was going to kick the daylights out of it—till daylight, if he felt like it.

The next day he continued the process of ensuring that everything was in place. The locals, especially the children, would be asking him later how things had gone. They all loved to hear his stories. He would tell them of the things he had seen while sober that had inevitably driven him to drink, and then he would tell them what he could remember of his subsequent escapades. Rollie Johnson was good-natured toward all except the despised magnolia tree. He had never hurt anyone or anything except for Mr. Gamble's new garage, which had been demolished during Rollie's drunken attempts to park a truck in it. (It seemed that the garage door would jump to another wall every time Rollie aimed the truck for it.)

Gnome in front of "Witch's Hut"
Courtesy of Daytona Museum of Arts and Sciences

The bungalow at Gamble Place
Courtesy of the Daytona Museum of Arts and Sciences

Rollie would eventually admit when he was teasing someone, but he swore to his deathbed that the pandemonium of Halloween night was true. He knew that it was not the locals who were moving the stone characters. They stayed away out of respect.

James Gamble was probably Florida's first regular winter visitor. He had seen the tract of land along Spruce Creek during a fishing trip in the late 1800s. The 150 acres, including the citrus-packing barn and five-acre orange grove, were bought for six hundred dollars. Rollie Johnson was hired as caretaker, and Gamble Place was built. For a short time, locals would cross the property line in search of fresh water. Mr. Gamble liked his privacy. Rather than raise fences, give warnings, or point firearms, he asserted his ownership and his character by digging an artesian well on the property line. There was enough artesian water for anyone who needed it. All were welcome at the well for free. In this and other ways, Mr. Gamble went from winter visitor to neighbor. When his yacht came up the Spruce for the winter, everyone turned out to dismantle the railroad trestle across the Spruce that blocked the yacht's way. The trains would simply have to take another route till March. Thus said Mr. Gamble, who owned the trestle, the railroad, and the trains.

The guests of Gamble Place included President William Howard Taft and captains of industry such as H. J. Heinz. All were invited for a day of hunting or fishing with Mr. Rollie Johnson as guide, cook, companion, and storyteller. Many of the guests returned, mainly to spend time with Mr. Johnson. He was the spice that set Gamble Place apart from any other country retreat in Florida. The evenings were spent on the front porch of the bungalow or inside playing cards. Then the guests would make the brief trip back to their winter homes at Daytona Beach.

No one stayed overnight except for Rollie Johnson. He was glad that the critters showed some restraint during full moons. All the statuary was back in place by the time the next day's visitors arrived. If there was no company, then he could continue taking care of the several acres of citrus groves near the bungalow. Nearly all the trees were orange trees, but Mr. Gamble had added kumquats. There were even a few circus trees, which had had limbs grafted onto them so that a single tree produced several kinds of oranges as well as lemons, limes, tangerines, guava, and kumquats all at once.

The groves prospered under Rollie's care except for the part adjoining the magnolia tree that Rollie hated so much. The tree was large enough to interfere with the orange trees next to it, crowding them so that they were sickly. More than two centuries old, the magnolia seemed determined to assert its magnificence by choking out whatever dared to grow nearby.

Rollie finally decided to cut down the magnolia tree but Mr. Gamble took him aside and declared, "I can always grow another orange tree or two, but it would take more than a lifetime to grow a tree that big." The magnolia remained, as did Rollie's determination to outlive it. He satisfied himself with doing whatever he could do to help the orange trees prosper, and to give the magnolia tree an emphatic kick whenever he passed by it.

The tree stayed. Guests came and went. The trestle was removed, replaced, and removed again. Rollie Johnson kept kicking the magnolia tree. These were the rhythms of Gamble Place till 1932, when Mr. Gamble died.

Another interruption came in 1937. Walt Disney released the movie *Snow White*. Judge Nippert, who had married Gamble's daughter, saw the show and had the idea of building a life-sized replica of the dwarves' house on the Gamble property. He hired a carpenter to draw up the plans. These were based on many viewings of the movie; later, some of the actual film cels were used. In less than three months the house was complete. Children could walk in and see the large fireplace, almost exactly like the one in the movie. They could go up the stairs and see the headboards of all seven dwarves. Nearby was a witch's hut, complete with a wooden standup of the witch herself. There was a wishing well and a building that looked like the dwarves' mine on the inside.

In 1938 Walt Disney himself came out to see the spectacle of children playing in *Snow White* come to life. He was so impressed that he sent life-sized dolls of many of the movie characters to be placed inside the Snow White house. No one knows if Mr. Disney heard about Mr. Johnson's frustrations with the stone characters that were coming to life.

Gamble Place, which had always been mostly a nature preserve, was donated to the Nature Conservancy in 1983. In 2000 it was deeded by the Conservancy to the Museum of Arts and Sciences in Daytona Beach. While we know something of the economic influence that people had on that area of Florida, the full extent of the influence of Gamble Place and Rollie Johnson is not clear. We know that in 1938 Mr. Disney was impressed by the sight of children playing within one of his movies come to life. We know of Rollie Johnson's insistence that the magic within Gamble Place had gotten a little out of hand. Whether there is a link or not, we know that Disneyland opened in California in 1955 and that Disney World opened in Orlando in 1971. Both parks have a Magic Kingdom. The Disney movies are well represented within them, with their characters walking about.

If the magic gets out of hand within the Disney empire, perhaps there is a Rollie Johnson assigned to deal with it. The original Mr.

Johnson died in 1934, still trying to outlive that old magnolia tree. The tree is thriving. Perhaps it felt safe in the care of the Nature Conservancy. But there are still reports that every Halloween night, a light is seen going to and fro within Gamble Place, swinging back and forth like Rollie Johnson's lantern. As for the stone gnomes, they're still there. No one else has seen them move or has had to give chase. According to unofficial reports from some of the groundskeepers, on the first of November the statues are almost exactly where they were the evening before.

Almost.

For those who want more evidence of Rollie's trials, the museum is planning to open Gamble Place to the public. People will have an opportunity to walk along the leaf-strewn path from the bungalow to the Snow White house and see what I saw: fanciful woodland gnomes made of stone along the paths. A few are broken and moss covered. Others are intact but weather-worn, with nothing at all growing on them. And as Rollie Johnson might have ruefully agreed, a strolling gnome gathers no moss.

Reaching Out

One of the more commonly reported manifestations of ghosts are cold or hot spots—areas where the temperature changes suddenly for no discernable reason. Sometimes people will report that something unseen has brushed past them, like a cool draft of air on an otherwise calm day. On being confronted by a ghost, no one seems to want to reach out to try to touch it; neither do the ghosts try to do the same. This brings up the question of how we look to ghosts—is their world as real to them as ours is to us—are the living but shadows in their world? Do they really vanish before our eyes, or do we vanish before theirs?

I have often thought that ghosts act as if they are dreaming and that we are part of their dreams. Sometimes when something unusual happens, we wonder or hope that we are dreaming. To see if something is real, we try to touch it. Such may be what happened in Pensacola over a century ago.

The firehouse was the Germania Hose Company. Except when there was a fire, things were quiet during night duty. Then the sounds started. Several times a week, vague noises would come from the walls of the station. The nightshift people would search the building high and low for the source of the noise but would find nothing. The most troublesome spot was at the back door, which would shake and sound as if something were trying to break it down.

The back door, like all the others, was kept locked and secured. Whatever was trying to get in didn't sound friendly. All night the noises would go on, except when the men would get up and check the building. When they went back to bed, the noises would start again.

Two men, Willie Britson and George Suarez, were on duty alone when apparently the unseen presence decided to check *them* out. The usual sounds started up. The men stayed in their cots, having gotten used to the sounds and knowing that all the doors were already secured. A rapping noise began moving along the walls.

A faint blue light, never before seen, then appeared in the midst of the room. It slowly formed the shape of a man dressed in white. Once formed, the apparition began moving toward the men as they lay in their cots. They were too frightened to move; besides, there would be some delay in getting out of any secured door. The ghost was now standing next to them as they buried their faces in their cots.

They felt icy cold hands touch their necks and deathly cold fingers wrap themselves onto whatever parts of their faces were exposed. The heat was being drained from their bodies. They were rendered too cold to move. Soon they were so numb from cold that they could no longer feel the ghost's hands. Slowly they began to warm up again.

After about half an hour they felt they could move. Peeking out from the covers, they found themselves alone. The noises had stopped. Their visitor, after reaching out and touching them, had left.

They still didn't sleep very well that night.

The Empty Bathtub

Near my office is a Denny's, where I sometimes go for lunch. It is about a hundred yards from my desk, which is about as far as one can travel in Florida without passing a church. If there's not a church with a steeple, there will be one without a steeple. Or a tent. Or anyplace that will do. In the middle of lunch, it was the Denny's.

At Denny's I looked up from my lunch and saw people all about me, many of whom knew each other. It was impossible to predict who would say hello to whom, for they seemed to be from all walks of life, both white folks and black folks of different ages. Then the preacher walked in.

He was a giant of a man, old and limping and with iron-gray hair. He had been burned black by many Florida days in the sun, but his eyes were clear and piercing, the eyes of someone who knew exactly why he was on this earth and who ordered his life accordingly, even to what he looked at. He gave a quick order to a waitress and moved from table to table. There was a hug here, a hand on a shoulder there, and a word of encouragement across the way. At table after table he served his people, till they good-naturedly shooed him to his own table before his food got any colder. It was a great show of respect and love between preacher and congregation. If the reverend ever died, many tears would be shed.

Dr. Teed didn't do so well. For having been the self-proclaimed leader of a religious movement, Dr. Cyrus Read Teed came to an ignominious end. His odyssey began in New York with his birth to very religious Baptist parents. The journey may have ended at the bottom of the Gulf of Mexico—nobody knows for certain.

His parents wanted him to become a minister, but instead Dr. Teed became a physician. Nothing in his earlier life prepared him adequately for his service to the Union Army during the Civil War. He could not reconcile the goodness of his parents' God with the evil and brutality he saw all around him. After the war, Teed developed his own religion. Conveniently, he himself was its center.

From his home in Chicago, he proclaimed that the Earth was hollow and that the universe was inside it. He gathered both followers and press notice. The Chicago newspapers ran article after article on him. He was characterized to the public as the leader of a cult that took the worldly goods from its followers and kept them enslaved through fear. Dr. Teed could not understand why the press was mocking him (the reason was that, for one thing, it sold a lot of papers) and so he fled to California.

There were newspapers in California too. Teed was now "Koresh the First," leader of the Koreshan Unity. California had not yet become the Granola State. The Western press deemed the self-proclaimed Messiah to be a fake whose church practiced nothing more than depriving the poor and ignorant of everything they had. Koresh the First found himself in another losing war with the press. He left again and traveled across his hollow globe, this time to southwest Florida.

In 1894 Dr. Teed and a few followers came to Estero, south of Ft. Myers, and began planning their New Jerusalem. Needing a place to put it, they eventually acquired a total of sixteen hundred acres by donation and purchase. Teed's headquarters were to be in the center of the city. The four-hundred-foot-wide streets would be in concentric circles radiating outward from the center. One quick look at a map suggests that there would be precious few circles before the streets hit the Gulf of Mexico and became half-circles, but the actual map that Dr. Teed used showed that the planning had been more carefully done than that.

Koresh the First declared that he had found his earthly paradise and invited all his followers to join him. Doing so would involve taking the train as far as Punta Gorda and then waiting for boat passage to Paradise. The doctor himself stayed at the house of an acquaintance in Punta Gorda when he was in town waiting for a boat.

Work on New Jerusalem was interrupted by Dr. Teed's death. Realizing that death was coming even to a messiah, however, he announced to his grieving flock that he would be resurrected on the third day after his last breath in order to continue work on New

Jerusalem. On December 22, 1908, he indulged in a torrent of curses upon the press and then died. Leaving his body in the nascent city's meeting hall, his followers set a watch for his resurrection.

After three days he was as dead as ever. His followers found it expedient to keep their watch farther and farther away from his body, which was getting so rank that even the skunks might have been complaining. With the passage of the third day, the Koreshan Church members were still patiently awaiting a resurrection. The local health department was uninterested in such spiritual matters and ordered a proper burial.

The church members placed the body of their leader into a galvanized bathtub and buried it under a concrete slab at the south end of Ft. Myers Beach. Days of waiting dragged into weeks and months. Instead of waiting to see Dr. Teed rise up in glory from his resting place, the thought was to provide a guide for him in case he awoke disoriented and needed directions back to New Jerusalem.

The day eventually came in which his followers were unable to keep watch over his tomb for lack of scuba gear. A monster of a storm struck in 1921 and washed away the entire southern tip of the island. The bathtub was nowhere to be found. If Koresh the First does rise, he will apparently do little more than momentarily confuse a few sharks.

Afterwards there were numerous reports of sightings of his ghost. Many were at the house in Punta Gorda where he had often stayed. No actual eyewitness ever came forth. The reports were always from a friend of someone who claimed to have seen him. The house in Punta Gorda was torn down in 1961. Whether it was because of a spirit, or because it had been well constructed, the house reportedly resisted its destruction. Every board shrieked like a banshee as it was pried from the others. Those who watched felt a strong presence within the home, and chill after chill as it was torn to pieces. Whatever spirit was there is now homeless, and the local neighborhood has reported sightings of a wandering ghost.

South of Ft. Myers, there is a state historic site about the Koreshan Unity near US 41. It is all that remains of New Jerusalem. A tour of the area's buildings and exhibits shows the serious side of the history of the Koreshan Unity: The people involved were talented and remarkably industrious. The policies regarding transportation and waste disposal were environmentally respectful ones that would not be adopted by other urban areas for decades.

As for the Koreshan Unity, the church doctrine contained the seeds of its own disappearance. They believed in celibacy.

Castillo de San Marcos

To get a graphic demonstration of some of the history of St. Augustine, take a chunk of Styrofoam and a ball bearing or marble. Firmly push the ball into the Styrofoam and leave it there. Raiders have tried the same thing with the thick coquina walls of the massive Castillo de San Marcos, the old Spanish fort that looms over much of St. Augustine. The raiders, using cannonballs, found that the coquina walls merely absorbed them and used them for decorations. The fort has lasted for over three hundred years. Cannon would probably still have the same effect today, although the port authorities and the National Park Service might be unreasonable about any cannon-laden ships sailing in and firing upon the fort.

The long history of the fort is generally honorable, but there are episodes of disgrace. One of them is a part of the fort's most enduring ghost story. It begins in 1784, when Colonel Garcia Marti and his beautiful young wife, Delores, arrived in St. Augustine and he assumed command of the fort. As Colonel Marti found himself inundated with his duties, young Delores noticed the dashing good looks of Colonel Marti's chief officer, Captain Manuel Abela.

Delores found that Captain Abela was much more available for her needs than her husband. As their love affair flowered, Captain Abela found himself serving his commander and the commander's wife in quite different ways. One day Colonel Marti and Captain Abela were studying maps together. Colonel Marti noted the scent of Delores's perfume on Captain Abela. He confronted the captain.

There were easy explanations for the immediate disappearances of both the captain and the lady. The captain, Colonel Marti said, had been reassigned to Spain. Delores had fallen ill and was convalescing with relatives in Mexico. For those who knew nothing of the affair, and for those who did, the explanations fit together and sufficed.

Almost fifty years later, a forgotten room was rediscovered within a wall of the fort's dungeon. In it were ashes and bones. As tour guides later told the story, the bones became human.

The tips for one tour guide got bigger when he added that there were two human skeletons. Soon the skeletons were chained to the wall, and a faint smell of perfume appeared. Those who get no tips know that the bones eventually proved to be animal bones. Common courtesy keeps this fact quiet as tourists pass the spot and announce that they can smell the perfume and see a faint glow.

As for the passions of the past, the real story of the Colonel and Delores has nothing to do with ghosts, and so it is the tale of another teller.

Lady's Walk

She was a young mom, at the end of her teens, with a perfectly beautiful little baby girl gurgling on her lap. "Yesterday she held her arms out to me, for me to pick her up. That was such a thrill," said the baby's proud mother.

"Is she your first?" I asked.

"No. My first one died when she was only a few minutes old. She was premature."

"I'm sorry," I replied. "That must have really hurt. Does it ever get better for you?"

"A little." She blushed, "I went kind of crazy after that. After I was discharged from the hospital, we buried her and I couldn't believe she was dead. Once I knelt down by her grave and started digging with my hands. I wanted to get to her and hold her just once more. People don't understand it, but I wanted so much to have her in my arms again."

I nodded. "Did your family help you? How about the father?"

"Oh, they were mad at me. I was only sixteen when I got pregnant with her. And her father—I can't believe I ever got involved with him. He was real upset and cold when I told him I was pregnant. He didn't want the baby, even though she was our baby. He wasn't there when she was born. He was at a bar. When he found out the baby was dead, he went home with his friends and some beer and threw a party.

"A couple of times I've visited her grave and found tire tracks on it, like someone ran over it and then gunned the engine. I think he did it with his truck."

"Does anybody seem to care how you feel about your daughter?" I asked.

"Not really. I'm very lonely like that sometimes. People got mad at me for getting pregnant, but why take it out on her? She was my baby. She was human too. Nobody cared about her but me; maybe it's better that she died. But I don't talk about her. I keep it inside me, because all people do is tell me how terrible I was to get pregnant with her."

I didn't add to the chorus of condemnations, of course. I keep politics and medicine separate. It was my pleasure to tell her instead that her current baby was thriving well in her care. She probably still carries a lonesome, unanswered love within herself.

She has a kindred spirit on Santa Rosa.

Deadman's Hollow and Pirates' Cove are two of the colorfully named parts of Santa Rosa Island, off the Florida panhandle at Pensacola. Their names come from the Pensacola area's colorful and long history, especially the part that teems with pirates. The story of the Lady's Walk that begins at Deadman's Hollow is so old that the names of the characters have been lost. Only the names of the places and the Lady's Walk itself remain.

Pirates used Deadman's Hollow. They provided it with dead men because of the pirates' murderous ways and via the sharp sword of their captain. Vicious as he was, he was a handsome and dashing man with dark eyes and jet-black hair. He had but to cross the water to Pensacola to become a different man. In Pensacola was a beautiful young Spanish woman with whom he had fallen in love. To her, he was as gallant as he was handsome. She, who was brought up in proper Spanish ways, fell hopelessly in love with her dashing captain, whom she saw as more of a rogue than the cutthroat he was.

The pirate's gallantry may not have been a masquerade. He was used to taking what he wanted, but he was willing to wait, however impatiently, for his lady. Instead of stealing treasure with his men, he stole time with her. Their moments together were spent furtively. Her father would never have approved of the pirate his daughter loved. To her father, love was either a bonus or an inconvenience. The more valuable piece of merchandise was the daughter herself, whom he planned to give in marriage to an elderly Spanish don whose possessions would add greatly to the family wealth.

Eventually, the daughter was caught by her father while going to her captain. Furious, humiliated, and faced with the prospect of losing the old don's riches, he locked his daughter in her room. From her window she could look out at night and see her lover pacing back and forth on Santa Rosa Island. He could have gathered his men and raided the household as pirates do. Instead, the gallant captain played by the self-serving rules of jealous fathers and the wealthy Spanish. He did not have to wait long.

The lady escaped from her room with the help of a servant and hurried to meet her lover. Once again her luck was poor and she was intercepted, this time by the old Spanish don. In the sight of the jealous pirate captain, the old don embraced her warmly. The captain's rage was such that any time she was in the arms of another man was far too much time. He would never believe that she had been embraced unwillingly.

She excused herself from the don as quickly as she could and hurried to Santa Rosa Island, to Deadman's Hollow. There was no gallant rogue waiting for her there. Instead was a murderous cutthroat whose sword awaited its next victim. Her profession of love for him was still in her throat when he slashed through it. The last secret they shared was how easily he severed her head from her body.

He dragged her body to Pirates' Cove and flung it into the water. What happened to her head is no longer known. Neither do we know what happened to her pirate captain and whether his anger ever cooled. He is gone, like the lady's father and the old don. The rage, the greed, and the avarice, have lasted only in the memories of storytellers.

As for the lady, her love goes on. She believed that the love within her own heart would conquer all obstacles, overwhelm the evil around her, and reignite the passions of her pirate. The lady believes it still, because she knows her heart and not what she has been transformed into by the men around her. She has been seen during full moons. She rises silently from the water and glides slowly to shore at Deadman's Hollow. The blood has been washed from her white clothes. She walks to Pirates' Cove to wait for him, and then returns to the water. Perhaps one night a man will be there at the cove. He may hear the sand crunch softly beneath her feet as she patiently returns to the familiar spot. In the moonlight he will see the torn strips of flesh where her head has been hacked away. Her neck may throb as her heart beats in both patient and impatient anticipation. She will reach out for him and try to find someone to return her love, as her headless body holds him in a lover's embrace.

Seahorse Key

Sitting about three miles southwest of Cedar Key and named appropriately for its shape, Seahorse Key is now a national wildlife refuge protecting a group of endangered brown pelicans. It is closed to the public, although it is used as a marine biology research station by the University of Florida. There is a dune on the island, which is over fifty feet above sea level and is one of the highest points on Florida's gulf coast. An abandoned lighthouse is there. The only access to the island is by boat.

If one has nothing better to do, one can drift about offshore at night and watch by moonlight for Pierre LeBlanc to ride past on horseback as part of his nightly rounds. If it is LeBlanc, the horse will be a palomino. The palomino will have a head. The rider will not. Seeing this sight is a good way to stay sober.

LeBlanc was a pirate in the employ of the famous pirate Jean LaFitte. While delivering a shipload of horses to New Orleans, LaFitte left a palomino on Seahorse Key for LeBlanc to use while patrolling the island. LaFitte's sea chest full of gold and jewels was buried on the island in a secret location.

One day LeBlanc discovered a stranger on the island. The stranger was hunting snakes for their skins, which he sold on the mainland. LeBlanc was initially suspicious, but it became obvious that the man really was there to hunt snakes. They spent time swapping stories and drinking together.

LeBlanc soon trusted the stranger enough to let himself get drunk while the stranger restrained himself sufficiently to remain sober. The hunter followed LeBlanc as he swayed drunkenly about on the palomino. LeBlanc stopped and passed out at the site of the sea chest. He woke up to see the stranger helping himself to LaFitte's jewels. LeBlanc attacked the hunter with his cutlass. The stranger was able to wrest the cutlass from the drunken LeBlanc and to behead him with it. Then he pushed off from the island in his boat. As he pulled away, he saw the palomino pacing back and forth on the shore.

No one knows what happened to the rest of LaFitte's treasure. There are about a thousand brown pelicans there who aren't talking. There is also a spectral palomino. His headless master still carries a cutlass stained with the blood he shed while giving his life to guard the treasure. If any others come to help themselves to Jean LaFitte's jewels, they may find themselves pitted against a sober and angry pirate who has nothing more to lose.

Villa Paula House

The Villa Paula House was built in 1925. It was the first Cuban consulate in Miami. The consul named it after his wife, Paula. He is gone, but she may still be there. Paula is supposed to be a benign spirit. Unfortunately, there is evidence that she has company and that her company does not follow her example.

The house has had many purposes. It became a private home during the Depression, when bought by a Muriel Reardon. Since then it has been a senior citizens' home, a refuge for drifters, a physician's office, and most recently, a restaurant. The Villa Paula has probably seen the gamut of human emotions, and it has definitely inspired some emotions on its own. One of them is fear. For a long time, its reputation as a haunted place was such that some people crossed the street rather than walk on the sidewalk in front of it. The part of the reputation that attracted my interest was the needless cruelty.

Ms. Reardon was supposed to have hated cats. A later owner had three of them. They all died in the same mysterious way—as they walked through an iron gate in back, which was normally left open and unlocked, it would suddenly swing shut and crush them. This always happened on days when there was no wind.

These were the most appalling incidents, unless one hates cats. Of all the ghosts I've heard of, only this one seemed to enjoy killing. I've also heard of cats being sensitive to the presence of ghosts, getting upset and having their fur stand on end, and moving quickly to avoid something unseen. This malevolent spirit seems to be faster than the cats.

There have been other incidents, less threatening but still unsettling. A chandelier above the front porch fell. One owner heard noises in the kitchen. Upon investigation, the dishes and silverware were found scattered on the floor.

Once a bedroom door slammed shut. Initially it seemed to do so for no reason. Later it was found that the room had contained the piano that Paula had played. She habitually kept the door shut to keep the draft from her bare shoulders as she played.

Paula herself has been glimpsed. An apparition hurrying down a hall has been seen wearing a frilly Spanish gown, her hair pulled back tightly. The figure vanishes even as one lays eyes on it. High heels are heard on a backyard path, but when one investigates, no one else is there. At least the spirit has two legs—unfortunately, Paula died in the house from complications from a leg amputation.

It is no longer a surprise to answer a rapping on the front door only to find nothing and no one.

Cuban coffee has been smelled brewing in an empty kitchen. The dining room may have an aroma of unseen roses. Nowadays there may be many more pleasant odors; the building was recently bought at auction and there are plans to convert it to a restaurant. What would Paula think? Or should we ask, "What will she think?"

Watcher

Having just returned to Florida the night before from enduring subfreezing temperatures in Ohio, I woke up and plodded to the mailbox in my shorts, T-shirt, and sandals. I was grateful for the warmth, while real Floridians complained of the cold. A small boy, looking about four years old, was striding purposefully across the apartment complex on his way to something important. He saw me and changed course, intercepting me like a small and bulky missile. I said hello as he stopped in front of me.

His tone was respectful and patient. "You wouldn't be so cold if you dressed like me," he said.

"Oh?"

"See? My mommy dressed me with long pants and a sweater. And she put socks on my feet so they won't get cold." He looked me straight in the eye, making sure I had heard him. "You should wear socks and a sweater too, so you can be warm like me."

"Well, of course I will. I'll go back to my apartment right now and do just that," I assured him. "Thank you for your help."

"You're welcome!" He went back on course to his other business, whatever it was. There was a tight little smile on his face. It was mid-morning, and he had already done his good deed for the day, helping an old geezer who obviously hadn't known any better. I returned home; winced at all the bills; and changed into long pants, socks, and a light sweater. I pocketed a can of mosquito repellent before getting into my car and driving to Everglades National Park. There was another little boy on my mind. This one had been on foot also, but not in the midst of the well-manicured grounds of an apartment complex. This one had bolted into the green wilderness of the Everglades ninety years before, hoping that whatever waited ahead of him was less terrifying than what he had been forced to do on Ed Watson's farm.

He had run as quickly as he could also run quietly, staying out of sight and earshot. He picked his way through the patches of grass that were too dense to show the rattlers and other venomous snakes that slithered on the ground beneath. He had waded through fresh-water streams as they met the Gulf, hoping that the water was too salty for the alligators that might be hidden in the muddy water. He had scampered over the clumps of mangrove roots that snapped underneath his weight and threatened with every step to snap his ankle as well. After a few miles, he would be able to rest briefly. He knelt down amid the painful clouds of mosquitoes, the poisonous snakes, the hungry alligators, and the sawgrass that slashed his skin; sharks prowled the coastal waters nearby. If no one had followed him to drag him back, he would be relatively safe. When he was afraid to rest any longer, he would run some more. On a flight that would eventually cover at least ten miles through the green wilderness, he was journeying northwest. I was driving southeast. Ninety years and ninety miles apart, we were closing in on the same place: Smallwood's General Store on Chokoloskee Island.

The road through Everglades City that ends in Chokoloskee is as far south as one can drive along the Gulf Coast of Florida. It comes off that coast onto a causeway to Chokoloskee Island. Once on the island, the road ends as a tight loop in the dirt next to Smallwood's General Store. One can get out of the car after parking along the loop and, unless distracted by the ravenous mosquitoes, contemplate standing where Ed Watson died as violently as he had lived.

Edgar Watson showed up unannounced in the area around the turn of the century. He built a two-story house for himself and his family on a mound near the Chatham River and made a living for himself trapping alligators, fishing, and hunting. He also cleared forty acres of the best farmland in the Everglades and grew a number of crops, including sugar cane. Although business would take

Smallwood's General Store in present times

him into the surrounding settlements at times, he had little else to do with other people. He never turned his back on anyone. What few words he said were said politely, but he always seemed nervous. His manner gave rise to a number of stories about him. The tales all seemed to involve Ed Watson having killed someone. His wife and three children were well liked, even though folks were wary of Mr. Watson himself.

The boy was especially wary. He was still trying to understand what kind of people were in the area. They did not do the things Mr. Watson did, but neither did they avoid him.

The first body was found in 1910. No one knew where Watson was at the time, but the body of the old woman was floating down the river from the area of his home. She had been carved open and her lungs and intestines removed, apparently to keep the air in them from helping her body float. It would not have had to sink much to be out of sight, although fishermen did eventually find her.

I could see the problem in finding her when I was on the National Park Service's boat tour of the western Everglades' Ten Thousand Islands. Even well offshore amid the mangrove clumps,

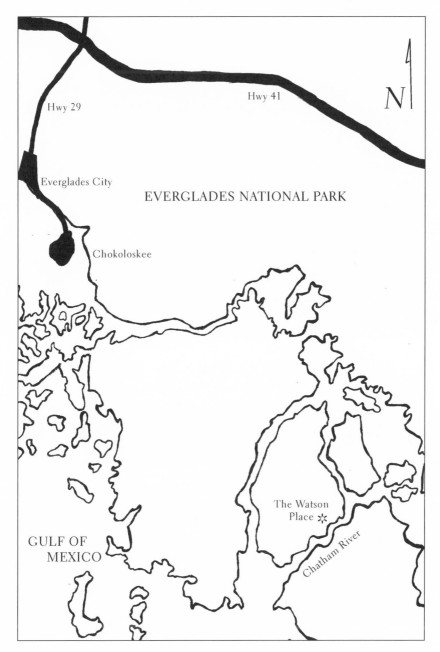

Map of the west Everglades
Drawn by Tory Powell

one can only see about a foot into the water. Muddy as it was, for us the water had pleasant surprises. Dolphins would sometimes leap out of it to play in the wake of our tour boat. They would turn sideways as they fell back into the water. Otherwise their snouts might get anchored in the mud. Even amid the Ten Thousand Islands, the water was shallow. Our boat, the *Manatee II*, drew three feet. The water was four and a half feet deep nearly everywhere we went. That meant we only had a foot and a half of clearance. We would not be able to tell if the boat sank, except that we would be at a dead stop.

Nevertheless, the Coast Guard has its rules. The boat had a life jacket for each crew member and passenger. There were three life rafts already inflated on top of the cabin. If the boat sank, we adults were to dutifully put on our life jackets, put the children in the life rafts or on our shoulders to keep them dry, and walk back to shore, towing the children behind us.

As the fishermen towed the old woman's body to the sheriff, they showed the body to some locals gathered at Smallwood's store along the way. The fishermen slowly went on their grisly journey. Gossip traveled faster. People compared observations—men, women, and children had been seen over the years going toward Watson's cane fields. Presumably they were migrant workers who drifted through Florida from farm to grove for one season or harvest at a time. No one had noticed the woman leaving for Watson's fields, but everyone now realized that she was the first person seen coming back.

The boy had been silent and watchful since arriving in the area, still trying to understand what kind of world he had come to. Reassured, he volunteered that he had escaped from Watson's farm after seeing Watson shoot other workers and then either bury them or gut them so that their bodies would sink when thrown into the water. The boy had been forced by Watson to help bury parts of some bodies while other parts were fed to the alligators. As the alligators prospered, so did Ed Watson. He had found an efficient way to keep from paying his migrant workers after the harvest was done.

If anyone had asked the obvious question, "Son, where are your parents?" the answer is not recorded.

The sheriff armed a posse and set out for Watson's place. Mrs. Watson and the children were visiting Chokoloskee and staying with friends. The posse found themselves standing on a huge, unmarked mass grave. Each man had to do little digging to find whether he was standing on a skull or the remains of an arm or leg. Other workers and their families who had been hired and then fired upon were found in the river. Upon returning, the sheriff set a watch for Ed Watson. They waited for him to come ashore someplace to transact his usual business, a transaction which many people decided would never take place.

Word came that their target was coming to Smallwood's General Store. An armed group watched Ed Watson's boat pull up a few yards from the stilts that keep the store above flood tides. They told him not to try to go into the store. Watson called what he thought was a bluff, stepped from his boat, and raised his shotgun. The posse's guns opened fire and kept firing till the men were satisfied that Ed Watson was the deadest man in Florida.

There would be time enough later for him to have a fair trial, if anyone were so inclined.

The gunfire has died down. Smallwood's General Store is now "Historic Smallwood's Store." One can still find the most modern mosquito repellents there. I have been in older trading posts but no friendlier ones. Except for a few tourists and the hum of mosquitoes, there is no sound but the gentle lapping of water beneath the stilts.

Three miles away, a walk along the clean streets of Everglades City is even quieter. Appropriately, the stains of the past have been taken away within the walls of an old laundry building, which now houses the Museum of the Everglades. I thought it was easily worth the suggested two-dollar donation. It was also where a gracious volunteer told me of the screams that are sometimes still heard at night from the swamp. They usually sound like those of a woman. The volunteer heard them when she was younger. She was not certain what other parents had told their children. Her own father had said that they were only the cries of a Florida panther.

The Watson house before its destruction
Photo used by permission of Lynn McMillian of the Smallwood family

I found it curious that a father would reassure his children that whatever was outside was only a mass of fur, fangs, and claws that could rip them all to shreds within seconds. Perhaps he believed it himself, or wanted to.

The Watson family tried to stay at their family house briefly after Ed's death. After they left, another family came and found that blood had appeared on one of the inside walls. Nothing could get it off. They tried to keep the farm from deteriorating, but no matter how hard they worked, the forty acres were slowly being reclaimed by the swamp around them. Even on the ground that they could keep cleared, the poisonous snakes were inexplicably getting more numerous.

By the time a nameless old woman arrived, the family had abandoned the house and moved on. She subsisted as best she could till she looked out a window one night.

There were lights about—glowing lights that floated above the ground and moved slowly, if at all. There were shadows and times when the lights themselves would pass behind something, only to reappear on the other side. Were the lights moving, or were there things moving among them? Whatever these things might have been, some of them were too tall to have been animals. Tall or short, many had limbs like trees. But trees didn't move—they were supposed to stay as fixed as the blood on the wall near where she stood.

She knew about swamp lights, but she was not used to the dark forms that seemed to lurk about the house as she peered from inside, alone. On the day that she could stand it no longer, she cut or burned down all the trees that grew close to the house, except for one that she left as a marker.

That night she watched, peeking out the window when she dared. The lights drifted into view. Despite the removal of the trees, the dark forms were back. She saw them rising from the bare ground—here a headless body, there a pair of legs stumbled over an arm that dragged itself painfully over the dirt.

Before her eyes, Ed Watson's last crop was coming up.

Desperate, she lit a torch and hoped its fire would keep them away. There was only one of her. No one was anywhere near to help. There was more than one door, and certainly more than one window. If they got into the house, she could throw open a door and run, but any path would have to be through...them.

She turned and saw that the doors and windows were secured against the moving and mutilated figures, but *they were coming through the walls.* She ran and pushed the torch at them, accomplishing nothing but setting fire to the walls themselves. How much longer before an arm reached through the floor and seized her ankle like a vise? Or until something dropped through the ceiling on top of her?

She threw open a door and ran like the little boy had, except she was screaming of spook lights and spirits rising from the ground. Screams are still heard from deep within the Everglades, coming from a vast darkness where some stories are better left untold and others best left undiscovered.

Only rarely does anyone go near the Watson place now. It has been reclaimed by the thick greenery that carpets and covers that part of the world. The great metal bowl used for making sugar cane syrup is still there, as are some of the supports to the house. However, to see them up close, one must brave a wide river of snakes that slithers slowly and unseen through the dense brush. And among the snakes, there may be other things, things that are taking a long rest after collecting on an old debt.

Steeples and Spirits:
Bulletins from Churches

Old Christ Church in Pensacola

A church haunted by priests? Hoping that one or more of these ghosts would consent to an interview, I had to check this one out. At least they would very likely be benign.

There are a number of stories about Christ Church and its former schoolhouse, but the most interesting one involves a multiple funeral. An archaeology project had found the remains of three of the former priests of the church and removed their coffins with the remains inside. The remains didn't lie quietly once the coffins were stored elsewhere (that is another story). But when the time came to rebury the priests, one of the people watching the procession got a surprise.

He saw the funeral procession go by with three people in it apparently mocking the ceremony. They were dressed as priests with black robes and carrying black books. All three were barefoot, in disregard to the solemnity of the service. Two of them got out of hand, talking and laughing and carrying on during the funeral. No one else noticed them except the third "priest," who was visibly embarrassed by his companions. The witness glanced briefly at the coffins; when he looked back, the three had vanished.

Then the witness asked others about what he had seen and found that no one else had noticed the three, though they had been so obvious to him. Later he found out that priests are buried barefoot with a prayer book.

Tarpon Springs

In the early 1970s, thousands of people made their way to Tarpon Springs by whatever routes they could. They headed for Florida's Gulf Coast and went north from Clearwater or south from cities above Tarpon Springs, eventually leaving their cars to join a long line that ended downtown on Orange Street. At the beginning of the line, each person would step through the main entrance of the Greek Orthodox Cathedral of St. Nicholas. By that time each person had probably heard that Tarpon Springs was a sponge-fishing settlement in which one third of the population was of Greek descent. They may have heard that St. Nicholas was the patron saint of fishermen and all others who work upon the seas. Learning such things was a way to pass the time until one stood inside the cathedral's main entrance and in front of the weeping icon of St. Nicholas.

The icon is an oil portrait of St. Nicholas. It is approximately three feet tall and is enclosed by an ornate frame that forms an airtight seal around the glass, which is pressed tightly against the painting itself. On December 5, 1970, a woman cleaning the church noticed that drops of water had appeared around the eyes on the portrait. The drops apparently came and went over the next several days. As witnessed by some of the parishioners, the droplets were forming under the glass. On December 14, the droplets were seen by Father Elias, the church pastor. As the skeptical pastor called in a carpenter to inspect the icon and its frame, the tears were seen by more and more people the following day. The carpenter found that the case was airtight. With condensation still suspected to be the cause, the icon and its case were moved into the sunlight. The tears not only continued to form but became a steady flow. There was a steady flow of people lining up to see the icon as well.

Not surprisingly, there were questions as to the meaning of the tears' appearance. Father Elias did not commit himself to an interpretation. After notification by Father Elias, the Archdiocese in New York City described the event as a "phenomenon beyond human comprehension." Archbishop Iakovos, primate of the Greek Orthodox Church of North and South America, came to see the icon and commented, "This may be a sign of the way Eternal God conveys His message to the believer." Church authorities have still not concluded what the tears' appearance means.

Sometime in early 1971, the flow of tears stopped. They started again twice thereafter, always during Christmas season. They were last seen on December 8, 1973.

I made an appointment to spend some time with the dean of the cathedral, Father Tryfon K. Theophilopolous. I asked him about the meaning of icons in the Greek Orthodox Church, since there were so many of them.

"The Church began using icons to explain its lessons in its early days—the days of the Apostles. Pictures were needed as symbols because so few could read or write. The icons are not worshiped. They are venerated or respected because of who they represent. An icon of a saint reminds us of the saint's life, and we are inspired by the way that person lived," he explained.

I wondered aloud if the "weeping icon," regarded as miraculous by many, might not deserve special treatment or veneration.

"Icons have no power in themselves," he replied, "including this one." I was fascinated by accounts he gave of miracles involving icons or statues in the 1,966-year history of the Church. As he pointed out, however, Orthodox Church members knew that the icons were nothing more than aids to the more important matters of learning and living Church beliefs.

He then invited me to see the weeping icon for myself. It is just to the left as one steps through the main entrance to the cathedral. It is truly pressed hard against the glass of its case; I cannot imagine

The "Weeping Icon" of St. Nicholas—tearstains can be seen on the beard

how condensation could have made the tracks that these drops of water made. The tracks are easily seen. They are about the width of a pencil eraser, or the width of a tear's path on a human face. They originate from the halo around St. Nicholas' head, as well as his crown and his face. Along each one's path, the painting has been discolored.

As I studied the icon, something seemed odd about the tracks. Closer inspection showed me something that had never been mentioned in anything I had heard or read about the icon. I went back to the office and asked Father Tryfon about it. He said that no one had ever brought it up before, and that he had never noticed it himself.

As it happens, the following week I met a family who were members at the cathedral and they had never heard of what I had noticed either: the tear tracks on the sides of the painting fall straight down, as would be expected from the effect of gravity and the fact that the painting is uniformly flat. However, the tracks on the face *follow the contours of the face. They curve inward on his cheeks toward the chin, around his nostrils, and then fall straight down from his face.*

As I had been assured, the icons of the Greek Orthodox Church have no special power in themselves. What *really* happened in the early 1970s in Tarpon Springs is not that the icon began weeping, but that in front of thousands of witnesses it changed from a portrait of St. Nicholas to a representation of a weeping St. Nicholas …a live-action demonstration.

What were the tears about? No one yet admits to knowing what the message was. I know that I learned a lot about icons from it. There was much to think about as I indulged myself by going down to the docks where the sponge fleet anchors. Shortly afterward I was in the Hellas Restaurant with my mind on more worldly matters. Halfway done with a plateful of the best Greek food I've ever had, I wondered how many Greek pastries I dared bring home from the restaurant's adjacent bakery.

Three tables over, an older waiter with an obvious zest for life was gently teasing two small boys who had not been able to finish their meal of chicken fingers. As he filled a take-home box with their leftovers, he asked, "Do you know how hard it is to find chickens with fingers?"

I had to laugh. I did not know the answer to the question and did not want to know. Especially not in Tarpon Springs, where everyday life includes the miraculous.

St. Paul's Episcopal Church

Sometimes a simple solution will present to a difficult problem. Skeptics may reject the solution as being too simple, too easy, and certainly too convenient. One might suspect that the skeptics enjoy arguing about the problem too much to accept an obvious solution. Like a broken clock, though, every once in a while the skeptics might be right. To see an example, consider going on one of Key West's Ghost Tours and make the stop at St. Paul's Episcopal

Church. After hearing the evidence, you can decide whether or not the venerable church is haunted.

The present structure is the fourth church building that has been built onto the property. The original church had had a small cemetery on the grounds. Construction of the present building required that most of the remains be disinterred and moved to Key West Cemetery. This was done with the permission of the families involved.

At least two graves remain. One was of a man named Fleming, whose family had donated the land on which the church stood. The only condition to this gift of land was that Fleming's grave stay on the property. It still does, and the headstone is part of the wall of the church. There is another grave that did not need to be moved. It is in the garden on the other side of the church from Duval Street. The headstone is flat on the ground, covering part of the plot.

There have been many sightings of a white figure moving slowly through the garden. It is only seen at dusk. It rises from the grave in the garden and walks slowly about. It is gone by the time night is fully established.

There are so many things to do and enjoy at Key West that few people have time or the inclination to watch a grave during sundown. Those who have happened by at the right time will notice a white goat that gets some relief from the afternoon heat by sleeping on the cool headstone. It gets up at dusk and wanders off for the night.

The mystery of the garden ghost might seem to have been solved, if one accepts that none of the witnesses knew a white goat when they saw one. Considering the amount of partying done on the island, this might well be true.

There is one more thing to account for. Recently a policeman found a homeless man in the garden cowering in terror. The man described a spot in the garden of numbing cold, far colder than any outside place should be at that time of night. He pointed out the location of the spot. The policeman had the same experience. Unseen ghosts are thought to cause spots of dramatic temperature changes. These are called cold spots or hot spots, depending of course on their temperature. Some think that walking through a cold spot means that one has walked through a ghost.

No goat could be seen. Is the garden of St. Paul's haunted? If not, then what would explain what has been happening there?

A *Side of*
Ectoplasm, Please:
Restaurants with Spirit(s)

Catalina's Place

C uba had been home to Catalina for twenty-one years while Florida was under British rule, but Catalina still remembered her childhood home in St. Augustine. Cuba was where she had met and married her husband, but Spanish Florida was where she had left behind ten years of her childhood.

In 1784, the year that Spain regained control of Florida, Catalina and her husband arrived at St. Augustine to get those ten years back. She followed the streets and her memories until she found her castle. It was a storage shed.

The British government had seized the house and converted it to such use. Along with Florida, the house had passed from the British to the Spanish government. Catalina and her husband petitioned the Spanish rulers for the return of the house. Even though there was no reason to turn the petitioners down, it took five years for the request to go through.

Catalina had long been dead when a series of sketches was done of the house in 1840. The sketches and the house's foundation survived the fire of 1887 that destroyed much of St. Augustine. From the pictorial record of its appearance, the house was reconstructed on its original foundation, using cement as a building material this time. The house remained a private home till becoming the first of a series of restaurants in 1976.

There are two things known about the ghosts of Catalina's old place: There is more than one of them, and at least one of them is particularly interested in fire. Whether this has anything to do with the fire that destroyed the first house is unknown.

The strangest incident recorded is that of the burning laundry basket. A basketful of uniforms and napkins, freshly cleaned and dried, was found with smoke coming from it one day. The contents were emptied out, but there was no fire, no cigarettes, no chemicals, nothing inside that could be smoking. Yet smoke had been pouring from deep within the pile of clothes.

On a number of occasions a fireplace has lit spontaneously, though there had been no fire in it for days, the ashes were cold, and there were no embers. Candles have lit by themselves. Light also comes from the electric lights, which have been found back on after all had been turned off in preparation for closing.

Despite the fascination with fire, the ghosts are considered friendly. The one seen most often is female. She has been thought to be Catalina by some; others call her Bridget. No one has ever gotten a good look at her face. That might be intentional on her part—she's been seen often enough that we should have an accurate freckle count if she had any.

A woman in a long, white dress has been seen frequently in the ladies' room on the second floor. She is normally seen in people's peripheral vision; upon their turning to get a better look, she is gone. Once she waited around long enough to walk through the bathroom door. She is seen in the second floor waiter's station too. There she appears in a mirror, always off to the side, and is gone when one turns to get a better look.

As if teasing everyone, she is seen from the back, going down the second floor hallway before vanishing. When the second floor is known to be empty of those who have discernible life signs, footsteps can be heard from upstairs by those down on the first floor. Men who pass by the second floor ladies' room have reported a strong odor of perfume from the room. Women who were assigned to keep the ladies' room clean and stocked have noticed that a small stack of tissues kept on the counter will be scattered all over the counter, sometimes several times a day.

There is a male counterpart on the first floor who has never been seen upstairs, but the two ghosts have never been known to interact. There are a few clues to the identity of the male. Supposedly a man died in the house during the 1887 fire. There is also a history of an ill man sent to occupy the empty house by his family in Ohio, who owned it at the time. His doctor thought the Florida weather would be better for his health. It wasn't, and the man died in the house soon after arrival.

The first sighting of the male ghost was by a woman dining on the first floor, who noticed him staring at her from where he was standing near the fireplace. She went to complain to a manager about the strange man in the old-fashioned black suit. The figure had vanished when the two of them arrived to investigate. Another diner asked a waitress who the man in the funny-looking black suit was; when the waitress turned to look, he had vanished. He has also been noted by some to be wearing a black hat.

The man is seen most often near the wine case. He was finally seen by a staff member going downstairs to the room where the wine case is. When she followed him and turned the corner to where the case was, he was gone. Either he had just *poofed* out of sight, or he had walked right through the case.

As stated above, the male and female ghosts seem to be unaware of each other. A clue to the identity of the female ghost came when the restaurant was renamed "Catalina's Gardens." Afterwards the woman's ghostly activity lessened significantly. Now the name has nothing to do with Catalina, but the managers report no odd activity at all. One can only guess as to why.

Perhaps the two spirits finally met, and wish some privacy.

Fireside Restaurant

It is not generally known when the Truitt family came to Brooksville. The last of this family died in 1973, when Miss Jean Truitt passed away.

Miss Jeanie was gone but not forgotten. Her portrait hung on a wall in her home, even after it was converted to the Fireside Restaurant. One could go into the restaurant and see what she looked like. Others found that at certain times, one could look into a certain back corner booth and see what she looked like, for her apparition could be seen there. Why she favored the booth is a mystery. It had not existed in her home.

Perhaps her appearing in the restaurant showed her sense of humor or was a gentle reminder that the restaurant operation itself was a guest in her home and existed with her permission. There were other little nudges that were thought to be her doing. No one had a problem with Miss Jeanie. At the most, odd things were ascribed to her, not blamed on her.

Soup could be made from scratch and be bubbling hot, yet get cold on the short journey to the table. A spoon that was minding its own business on a counter top would suddenly be enjoying the floor's point of view. The people in Brooksville took these things as a matter of course because everyone knew about Miss Jeanie. The sudden draft from nowhere was merely another reminder that they were not only paying customers in a restaurant but guests in her home.

Over twenty-five years have passed since Miss Jeanie passed on and ended the Truitt family. Time cools and darkens a glowing ember, and the years have seen less and less of Miss Jeanie. Nowadays one can go into the restaurant that was once her home, and not even the staff knows who she is or was. Ask the young people—they never heard of her. Ask the old folks—they remember hearing about Miss Jeanie a long time ago, but those memories have faded.

Now the Truitt family is truly gone. Miss Jeanie got a proper burial. As far as people knowing about her lingering spectral presence,

93

there is only ignorance, silence, and fading memories. Such is the departure and epitaph of a ghost.

Ashley's

Glasses and mirrors shattered in the bar, though no one was anywhere near it. Everyone was fighting the fire that had broken out in the still-unfinished building. No one could tell how the fire had started.

Years later, in the midst of the Great Depression, a young woman left the building in the company of a well-dressed gentleman. She had a tattoo on her right thigh, the initials "BK" with a noose around them. The tattoo was seen the following day, the only identifying mark on the burned and mutilated body of a dead young woman. Her young and unharmed face was seen again fifty years later reflected in the mirror of the ladies' room of the same building.

Glasses still break, whether from being dropped, vibrating off a shelf as a train rumbles by on the nearby tracks, or by committing suicide from a shelf well away from human hands. But the food is great in the bar and the atmosphere convivial.

The view of Ashley's from the street may not be as reassuring. Lights and movement can be seen inside when the building is supposed to be closed and empty. The Rockledge police have to deal with burglar alarms that go off and demand the usual fruitless investigation, and with finding nothing but lights that turn on by themselves and hearing whispers from empty rooms. A woman's scream was heard from the empty building once. There's never been evidence of a forced entry. Given the things that have happened there, mostly when the restaurant is closed, it's surprising that there's never been evidence of a forced exit either.

An investigation into yet another suspicious sighting of light and movement long after everyone has gone home would include the ladies' room. This is where a manager once used the facilities and noticed through the opening between stalls that whoever was next door was wearing old-fashioned, high-buttoned, high-heeled boots.

When she had finished and left her stall, she seemed to vanish, for the stall door stood open, but no one else in the restroom had heard her or seen her leave. One can come into the ladies' room via a door from the lobby and leave through a small corridor that goes to another door. Some people have felt a choking sensation while walking through that little corridor. If that does not make an investigating officer turn around and look back, perhaps the sound of a sink's faucet turning itself on will do so.

The officer might then carefully negotiate the stairs upward—people have often felt themselves pushed or shoved by some thing unseen on those stairs. A storage room on the second level has some quality that makes people nervous for no particular reason. These people include the ones who don't know about the phantom woman seen casually sitting at a desk by a waitress, and those who never heard another waitress tell how while reaching for something high on a shelf, she put her foot out for balance and kicked something invisible.

Upstairs is also where the old man lived a few decades ago. He had been given a room there in exchange for doing odd jobs around the building. He has not claimed any space upstairs lately, but he may still be trying to help out. Recently, one table's group complained about a long-overdue food order that had been taken by their waiter, an elderly man. No degree or course of study in restaurant management could help with this one—Ashley's had no elderly waiters at the time. (The staff that are now employed give excellent service. Whatever ages and genders are represented, they are all at least alive.)

Phantom shoves might be ignored as an officer rushes downstairs to check out the faint sounds from the area of the salad bar, but the sound will only be the sneeze guard rattling. (I found that the plate was bolted firmly in place when I visited.) It can be seen by the lights of the hurricane lamps that have lit by themselves. Hopefully the light will be good enough to help one avoid stepping on Ashley's moving pictures. These are hung on the walls, except when they fly off the walls by themselves and are found neatly stacked on the floor.

Front door of Ashley's

It's a good idea to move slowly through the kitchen. The exhaust fans have been known to come on by themselves, though no one has been within twenty feet of the switches. Besides, a jar was once witnessed flying off a shelf. Bread baskets that had been neatly stacked may be strewn about. Once the exhaust fans have been turned off and the air conditioning has been confirmed to be off as well, another cause will have to be postulated for the sudden gust of wind that sweeps through the restaurant before its main door is opened.

The officers may pause at the door before leaving as they hear their names called out from the empty lobby. They have gotten used to that little ploy. A glance behind them might show a little girl strolling past the salad bar. They don't waste her time (or theirs) trying to question her. No one knows what business she has there at that late hour. The police do know who she is.

She is the little girl who was killed in an accident on the nearby highway years ago.

Pizza Hut

As America's oldest city, St. Augustine has its share of ghosts lurking at cemeteries, houses dating back centuries ago, and …a Pizza Hut. There it sits on US Highway 1—a haunted Pizza Hut.

The site of the Pizza Hut was involved in the great fire of 1887 that devastated much of the city. The story is that a number of people died on that site: a mother and her children, including babies. A Spanish soldier is also thought to have died there, although not necessarily at the time of the fire. Because of the number of haunted buildings in the general area, it's possible that the soldier may have wandered in from someone's house. Psychics who have had trouble lately convincing a spirit to show itself may wish to take note—consider a medium Meat-Lover's Special on a hand-tossed crust.

The Spanish soldier has been seen passing through the kitchen area. There is an adult female spirit who often rattles keys. She herself is never seen, only heard. Sounds of children are heard in the back of the building, especially the sounds of babies crying. A thumping is also heard sometimes in the back while it is empty, perhaps the echo of someone trying to get in or out of the building.

The spirits primarily make noises in the back, though they have free range of the restaurant. When the restaurant has been left darkened for the night after closing, lights will turn back on. Although Florida ghosts tend to ignore modern contraptions, the Pizza Hut ghosts have apparently discovered the jukebox. It is sometimes found playing long after being turned off in preparation for closing.

Are there permanent spectral residents within the Pizza Hut? Or, with the concentration of hauntings in the neighborhood, do some of the nearby spooks sometimes get a craving to hit the Hut? We may never know, unless they start leaving tips.

Homestead Restaurant

"Mrs. Paynter is very good to me. She's done nothing scary," said the staff member at the Homestead Restaurant. The two-story log cabin structure is a restaurant where one can sit back, enjoy the food, and spend a memorable afternoon hearing the staff's stories. Sometimes people might wonder whether even a gentle haunting is a plus or a minus for a business; in the case of this Jacksonville eatery, the spirit of Alpha Paynter is definitely a plus.

Mrs. Paynter operated a boarding house in the building about seventy years ago. The exact cause of her death, thought to have occurred away from the building, is not clear. Surprisingly, a psychic once went upstairs and had an overwhelming sensation that Mrs. Paynter had died a terrible death upstairs. History disagrees.

The ghost of Alpha Paynter may get some credit that she doesn't deserve. There's a friendly cat who showed up from nowhere and hangs around the outside, especially since the staff started feeding her leftover chicken. Some have joked that the cat is a reincarnation of Mrs. Paynter. There has been a little shelter built for the cat outside for use during inclement weather, but oddly, the cat will occasionally appear in the restaurant after hours. This is even when the doors have been closed and locked while the cat is outside. No one has any idea how the cat has gotten in.

Of course, the discriminating and demanding reader may want more evidence of a haunting than a sly little cat. Decades of haunting have provided the staff of the restaurant with a myriad of stories. There is the office worker who found herself out of money one day and who was distraught till a manager learned what her problem was and offered to loan her what she needed. The girl said she only needed twenty dollars. The manager replied that she would just give her the twenty, and she was not to worry about paying it back. Before the manager could get the money from her purse, however, she stopped to pull some linens from the dryer. Amid the linens was a twenty-dollar bill.

No one ever reported it lost. Not even the ghost of Alpha Paynter. An apparition of a woman has been seen many times by different people in different parts of the restaurant. The ghost has never done anything to scare anyone, even when unseen.

One evening, Marta was taking down drapes to wash when she tripped and started to fall. "There are six tables where I was. I put out my hand as I fell and the top of one table just flew up against my hand and caught it. It kept me from falling. The tabletop just came up by itself. Before we opened the next day I asked some of our workers to check that table because the top was loose. It had come off its base when I fell the night before.

"They all got real quiet and looked pale. They told me that they had stacked the chairs on all six tables the night before and blown out the candles that were on the tables. There was nothing wrong with the table I was talking about, but after they had stacked the chairs on it, the candle lit by itself. It was just that table and that candle."

If there were a contest for the most feminine touch added to a building by a ghost, the winner would be Mrs. Paynter. One young woman who worked in the upstairs office noticed that for several weeks, whenever she was in that office, she could hear children playing outside. "It sounded like there was a playground right on the parking lot. This happened every day, but only for a few weeks. I never heard the sounds when I was outside the office. I was surprised, because I thought that the kids should be in school or something. Then I would go outside and look—no children, and the sounds were gone.

Homestead Restaurant (interior)

"We moved away for a short time after that, and then I found out I was pregnant. I never heard those playground noises anywhere else, until we moved back a few years later. I went back to work here at the restaurant. One day I heard the noises again. Same thing—children playing and laughing and talking, but only while I was in the office. Then I found out I was pregnant again."

Unlike the people at many haunted places, the staff at the Homestead doesn't complain much about feeling an invisible presence close by that is watching them. Mrs. Paynter doesn't seem to want to cause a commotion. After all, the former proprietress of a reputable boarding house knows something about hospitality.

She is no shrinking violet either. Once a manager who had yet to experience any unexplained happenings said out loud that he wished that Mrs. Paynter would make herself known. Then a woman's voice could be heard calling from the second floor. Twice.

Everyone who heard her looked at each other, knowing that they were the only people in the building and that they were all standing on the first floor.

*They Never Sign
the Register:*
Other Public
Haunted Places

Biglow-Helms House

Maybe they didn't want to mess with anyone who could lift a five-hundred-ton house. The Biglow-Helms house in Tampa is quiet now. Compared with its past, its present is probably downright dull, but that may be the way its current occupants, the tangible ones, like it.

The house was built in 1908 on the corner of Bayshore and Gandy Boulevards by Gilas Leland Biglow. He had come from Brooklyn in 1884 and later served on Tampa's first city council. He died in 1917. His widow sold the gray-stone mansion to Dr. John Sullivan Helms, who converted it to the first private hospital on Florida's west coast. Since then the edifice has also been an artist's home and studio, and later an office complex. Sometime in the past decades, visitors started reporting seeing Gilas Biglow's apparition in the house. After its hospital days, the cries of phantom babies were heard from empty sections of its ten thousand square feet. Other visitors reported a feeling of being watched, not knowing if it was by Mr. Biglow or ethereal babies needing their ghostly diapers changed.

The real creepiness came from the live population. After the death of the artist in the 1960s, the house sat unused for almost twenty years. It collected dust, grime, graffiti, satanic symbols, and blood on its walls that suggested satanic rituals. The Swiss family that eventually bought the mansion had the house blessed by a priest as the ink dried on the purchase papers. Later, all five hundred tons of the gray-stone structure were moved to the front of the lot to make room for twenty-four luxury apartments. The mansion had plenty of room for offices.

According to people nowadays, nothing weird has happened at the Biglow-Helms house in recent years. A ghost from the 1800s might certainly be impressed with whatever is capable of moving the house. Perhaps the ghosts were disturbed enough by the bloody rituals that they folded their sheets and stole silently away. The reason for the cessation of ghostly activity at the Biglow-Helms house is now known only to the ghosts, wherever they reside in the past.

Community Development Corporation

Perhaps a music major from a nearby college was exploring the frontiers of contemporary music. If he or she was doing this in the office building, no one at the Community Development Corporation, which owned the building, was informed.

One would think that a federal agency that quietly occupied a Miami building would be overlooked by any musician in search of something new and unexplored. Or maybe the office staff were just caught up in a story whose ending has not yet been written.

Part One began in 1981. The CDC was not the only occupant of the building. There were other business offices, and yet there were still more rooms that lay dark and empty. The rooms were quiet, too, until low voices began calling from them. The office workers didn't work in the dark and empty rooms, though; they worked in the brightly lit ones. If there was anything creepy in the dark rooms with the voices, then a closed door was an easy solution.

However, the same closed doors had doorknobs that would jiggle. The knobs would stop jiggling when one gripped them and opened the doors—but when the doors were opened no one was there. Then "they" waited till some time after the doors had been closed to jiggle again. The knobs might have been vibrating in time with the furniture, which sometimes shook inexplicably.

In the meantime, the other offices were doing just fine. No one else had seen the black-hooded figure that a CDC staffer sometimes glimpsed in the hallway before the figure vanished. No one else had seen the flashing lights. Papers disappeared and reappeared, but every office has its absent-minded person whose working hours are spent more in searching than working.

Part Two was announced by the music. Guitar music could be heard from one of the conference rooms late one night. That was no problem—one of the fund-raising coordinators had stayed late and was relaxing during a break with his guitar. As he played, he heard the other music. It was a pipe organ. Nobody, of course, carried a pipe organ to work to relax with on breaks. The music was unmistakable, but no one was playing it on a player of any type, and the building had no organ and was blocks away from the nearest church.

The pipe organ sounded again and again. It came most frequently on Sunday nights. The music was nothing anyone could recognize, even in the other office where it was being heard. It sounded like hymns were being practiced, but they were unfamiliar ones. Ironically, the "hymns" inspired the growth of collections upon the office desks—collections of icons, crucifixes, and vials of holy water.

As if drawn to the symbols of holiness, the music kept coming. There was an ominous air about it. It would build toward a climax, then stop abruptly. Part Two of whatever was happening was evidently not the ending. Even minor mysteries, like the radio that turned on by itself and the roll of toilet paper that rolled across the floor by itself, were caught up in the greater question of, what was happening?

The music suggested that there was a Part Three. It kept coming, building in a crescendo toward a climax that has yet to come. It played as desks were being cleaned out. It sounded as the furniture was being moved elsewhere. The hymnlike melodies soon found no icons, crucifixes, or vials of holy water. After little over a year, the CDC had moved. Then the music and the voices stopped. What lies in wait within Part Three, no one knows.

There is now an intermission.

DeBary Hall

Have you heard any stories about DeBary Hall's being haunted or about strange things happening there?" I put this question to a number of people in DeBary. Every time, I got the same negative answer. No one has heard a thing. Maybe it is not haunted. It doesn't look very haunted to me.

Built in 1871, DeBary Hall is still being restored. It is a mid–nineteenth-century Southern plantation home with twenty rooms, a spacious porch and upper balcony, and a white exterior. It's not exactly your dilapidated, grim, and dingy morass of menace that I associate with old haunted houses.

But a little research turns up stories…

A worker for the Volusia County Parks and Recreation Department was trimming trees near the empty hall when he saw an attractive teenaged girl watching him from a second-story window. She was wearing a dark coat, as dark as her hair. Then she vanished. The worker told his story to a female volunteer in the building two days later, and he was stunned when she opened a closet door and showed him what was inside: It was the same coat. It belonged to a DeBary Hall board member. No one could explain how the coat got from the closet to the upstairs window, or who was wearing it.

The worker's supervisor has had eerie experiences too. Walking through the empty building, one can expect the usual unexplainable and hard-to-describe noises that are common in old buildings. But the supervisor heard the unmistakable sound of a slamming door on a calm day. She also saw a door opening by itself.

A Canadian writer once asked permission to spend the night in the house. She didn't get it, but she did slip onto the grounds one night and sleep on the veranda. Late that night she woke to a faint vibration within the floor beneath her. A loud moan sounded from within a few feet of her. She turned to look, and saw a "pale, fleet movement through the window, gone before I could define it."

Two teenaged girls who have stayed with their aunt at the caretaker's house have reported hearing footsteps from the empty upstairs and seeing an apparition in white at one of the upstairs windows. Two yard workers have also seen a figure in white in an upper window. They described a man in a white suit.

The question remains: DeBary Hall, haunted or not? If so, by whom? There's no history of violent death there. One young woman did die in the house, but she wasn't a teenager.

For all I know, there may be ghosts in there asking other ghosts if they believe in people.

The Muse of Maitland

> I stood at the gate of life and said, Give me a light that
> I may go safely into the unknown. And a voice replied,
> Go out into the darkness and put your hand into the
> hand of God. That will be to you better than a light and
> safer than a known way.
>
> — *Inscription on a wall*
> *at the Maitland Art Center*

The Orlando metropolitan area includes Maitland on its north side. After entering Maitland and turning onto Packwood Avenue, one finds the avenue turned to cobblestones on the approach to the Maitland Art Center. The center is a complex of studios, living quarters, galleries, offices, and gardens begun in the 1930s by Jules Andre Smith. A brochure says that the center is, among other things, "a perpetual memorial to its founder, Andre Smith, who believed art to be a constantly changing reflection of the present time rooted in the events of the past."

There is little question about the "constantly changing reflection" part. Almost every step through the gardens designed by Smith reveals a previously hidden sculpture or carving. The complex is filled with small studios with locked doors and uncovered windows. There are corners, alcoves, and no end of nooks and crannies. No matter how many other people are on the grounds, each step gives the observer a new and unique perspective and the sense of having discovered a carefully placed secret.

As the brochure says, some of the secrets are rooted in the past. Historical events come to life within the galleries' exhibits. There are reports that Andre Smith himself, founder and original designer of the center, still manifests himself in a number of ways, despite the inconvenience of having been dead a number of years.

It is perhaps inevitable that, in a collection of art studios within an art research complex, those artists who are looking for inspiration might sense the presence of Andre Smith. But how would one explain away the painting of Smith that I saw to my left when I entered the center's gift shop from outside? One of the resident artists had come into a gallery one night and, thinking that he was alone, investigated an odd sound. He found an apparition of Andre Smith, who had been dead for two years, standing amid rings of color like clouds. The apparition disappeared. The artist painted what he had seen. I had heard about the painting and the story behind it. I had expected that the colors would be bright reds and blues and such. Instead they are rings of dark and somber hues such as the ones Smith had used in depicting scenes of industry and war.

Some artists have heard an unseen man's voice whispering suggestions or have felt their brushes guided by an unseen force. One artist heard the disembodied voices of Smith and a woman discussing the work he was doing; others have changed their approach or technique in response to a gentle suggestion from nowhere and then found greater critical and commercial success.

Other presences have been noted as well. A bride appears in several of Smith's paintings. A figure in an old-fashioned bridal dress was seen behind a couple at the altar during a wedding held in the center's chapel. More run-of-the-mill, almost obligatory incidents happen at the center, as if a ghostly beginner were using a check-list—rocking chairs rock by themselves, and unexplained tapping sounds have been picked up by tape recorders left on at night.

A creative artist would not be expected to blindly follow a check-list, whether in life or in an afterlife. A bust of Andre Smith occupies one end of a room where he liked to meditate. The room reputedly is octagonal. There are still eight sides, but perhaps because of remodeling it is mainly rectangular, with an angled blind end and a three-sided outcropping that makes room for more exhibits. Two reporters who went into Smith's former place of meditation felt cold chills while there. The room has no drafts, but perhaps the chills came from reports of those who have seen the bust move, grin, or even wink. The bust wouldn't perform for me, even in my peripheral vision while I studied the other exhibits.

I was not surprised. Art is not created to live up to my expectations. Yet the center itself is a work of art—could it be that there are aspects of it that go beyond the purely visual? The place is rich with textures to be touched, and there are all kinds of changes in the grounds for those who would notice them. Flowers and grass—here today, gone tomorrow—are woven with wood and stone and metal. Permanence is blended with impermanence. Change comes daily and even hourly in some places within the garden, but far more slowly to metal gates and stone carvings. Perhaps whatever remains of Andre Smith is determined to add a new spiritual dimension to his creation.

Transient things include the smells. Despite a no-smoking policy, cigar smoke is sometimes noted. Smith smoked cigars. The odor is rarely, if ever, noted during the summer months, during which Smith would go to cooler climates.

There are also the sounds. While artists have heard whispers and other conversation from beings unseen, a thump-step rhythm was once heard while a display of Smith's work was being arranged. The director was setting up the display himself and could hear the thump-step behind him, going from canvas to canvas. Smith had a wooden leg. Sometimes he used a crutch.

There are sounds of something destructive happening, but no harm is ever done. Smith may have had a sly sense of humor. There are numerous reports of people alone in a gallery or workshop who have heard the sounds of paintings falling or of glass shattering behind them. Except for the artist who saw the apparition of Andre Smith ringed by colors, nothing unusual has been found after the sounds.

One story tells of harm being prevented. The floors of the galleries are not perfectly level or stable. They are on a foundation of wood instead of concrete. The ground beneath slopes downward toward a lake on the west side. There is a sensation of slight unsteadiness while one is walking through the galleries. It almost forces one to walk slowly. In addition, the ground is prone to flooding because of the sloping between two lakes. One teacher took down a display of student work and left the pieces collected in a corner on the floor for the night. This section of floor sits slightly lower than the rest of the floor because of the unevenness of the studio's foundation.

That night, it rained and rained, so much so that the teacher was not at all surprised to find the carpet soaked when she opened up the next morning. Heartsick at the thought of seeing the students' work floating in the low-lying corner, she was shocked to find it completely dry. Everything was still stacked in the corner, but there was a dry triangle in the carpet consisting of the corner itself and a visible line of dryness across which the water had been prevented from going. The question still remains: By whom or what was the corner kept dry?

St. Petersburg High School

April was the first teenager I got to know when I began working in Florida. Through her, Florida teenagers made a good first impression. Although she moved away shortly after we met, I will

St. Petersburg High School

probably speak of her when I am elderly, gone senile, and prattling incessantly of the past. When we spoke, there was always a sincere sweetness to her spirit that made my heart ache, wishing that there were more people like her of any age.

I once caught a glimpse of April while I was leaving home for the hospital. There was a sunset behind her. Her eyes were fixed on nothing in particular except the future. She was waiting for a ride to an athletic meet, her uniform gracing a body that somehow blended firm discipline and growing adolescent exuberance. It was more remarkable a sight because of what I knew about her.

When I was training to be a doctor, five incurable diseases accounted for most children's hospital admissions. Through no one's fault, she has three of them. She wears the responsibility for her own care as gracefully as she wears the uniform of her chosen sport. April will probably outlive a lot of doctors and nurses as they worry themselves to death about her.

Because I wish her all good things, I hope that she has teachers like Adrian Davis. It is fitting that Adrian Davis is remembered more for the teacher he was than anything else. In his thirty-five-year career at St. Petersburg High School, he taught such science subjects as biology, human physiology and anatomy, and honors marine biology. There is a long list of successful alumni of the school who were inspired and encouraged by him. As integral a part of the school's history as he is, it was with considerable difficulty that I found out anything at all about his lab assistants—many of whom were all the more elusive because they were invisible.

Mr. Davis required that to be a lab assistant in one of his classes, the student must have made an A in that class. In the 1950s, when teachers were allowed to do so, he preferred not to have girls as lab assistants—they tended to be repulsed by some of the preparatory work required for animal specimens. One year a girl asked to be a lab assistant. Although she met the grade requirement, he reiterated his males-only policy, but she was both insistent and sincere. Soon he felt like refusing her would be like refusing his own mother. Certainly the girl was persuasive, but she was also wearing Shalimar, which was his mother's favorite perfume. She got the job and became one of the best lab assistants in the years to come.

The year went well and she graduated. Tragically, it was not long after she started college that she was killed in an accident. It was an abrupt end to what was predicted to be a bright career in science.

Some time after her funeral, odd and unexplained noises were heard up on the third floor of the high school, in the attic rooms. Mr. Davis had developed the attic into a lecture room, a lab, and a long movie hall that contained his office and slide presentation materials. No explanation could be given for the giggles and whispers, until the day that Mr. Davis was teaching a class and heard a familiar sound coming from his office in the next room. It was a *squeak...squeak...* from his office chair.

"Someone was sitting in my chair," Mr. Davis related. His lab assistants would sit in the chair and grade pop quizzes, but he was puzzled, as he did not have a lab assistant that period. "I felt like one of the three bears with Goldilocks."

Mr. Davis excused himself from the class and went into the office, only to see an empty chair jerking back and forth abruptly as if someone had just jumped up from sitting in it. No one but Mr. Davis was in the office or the slide lab; no one had been seen or heard to leave. There had been no sound of footsteps. Nothing had brushed past him. From the area of the chair came the faint scent of Shalimar. He wondered whether his olfactory sense was playing tricks on him from so many hours of inhaling formaldehyde.

Had his first female lab assistant come back? If so, why the biology section of her high school, of all the places she had ever been? The mystery deepened later on during a class that was having a moment of silent prayer (this was before the Supreme Court rulings against prayer in schools), when all of a sudden a large section of shelves holding lab specimens crashed to the floor. Specimen jars shattered, liquids splashed, and a brain came rolling across the floor, coming to rest between one horrified student's feet. Somehow, amid the stench of fixatives and preservatives, Mr. Davis caught a whiff of Shalimar as the students left the lab in all directions. To this day at class reunions, he and many former students get a good laugh about this episode and what might have caused it.

Not surprisingly, he was wondering if he was imagining the Shalimar whenever anything odd happened. The next incident both deepened the mystery and answered part of it. Needing a former student's essay on bioluminescence, he asked a student assistant during first period to get it from the filing cabinet. The student wasn't able to find it. The student assistant for the second period couldn't find it either, and so on throughout the day though Mr. Davis knew the paper was clearly marked and could be easily found.

Mr. Davis looked for it himself after school. There the paper was, the first one filed under "B." It was pulled above the others and made as obvious as it could be. It was an "A+" paper and had been written by another trusted female lab assistant who had also died in an accident while attending college. He had attended her funeral a few years earlier. This time there was no hint of Shalimar. Was someone else drawing attention to herself?

By this time, Mr. Davis was wondering about a lot of things. Were the incidents the doing of guardian angels or of spirits who liked to play jokes on him?

Whatever was happening, there were still classes to teach and tests to give. In his classroom was an old ship's bell that he called his "cheating bell." Whenever he saw someone cheating, he rang it. Sometimes he would ring it just to unnerve and straighten out anyone who might have been cheating without his noticing. One day while he was standing well away from it, the bell rang firmly three times. Nothing was near it except the scent of Shalimar.

As helpful as his unseen assistants were, they were still students at heart. Mr. Davis had no second thoughts about challenging his students with the bane of students everywhere—the dreaded and despised pop quiz. On one occasion he had given one and had stacked the papers on a corner of his lecture desk while the class worked on the daily assignment. His lab assistants would later grade the papers in his office. He started his daily lecture. The air was calm in the windowless room. There was no draft or breeze from the door that was open to the hallway. Without warning, the papers rose from their stack, one at a time, in front of the whole startled class. They swirled in a funnel cloud of pop quizzes to the ceiling and downward, floating out the door to the far end of the third floor hallway from which a lab assistant retrieved them.

This memorable incident had an encore during a slide presentation about a coral reef. The slides in the projector's carousel were numbered, corresponding to a stack of cards on his lecture stand so that he could discuss the slides in order. Suddenly the cards flew up into the air and fell back to the floor as a mixed pile. This ended the day's presentation early, to the students' delight.

"Students who are now doctors, lawyers, and dentists here in St. Petersburg saw these things happen," says Davis. "There was no draft or wind. I still can't explain it."

Adrian Davis has since retired from a long and honorable teaching career. Laden with awards and cherished memories of his students, he has retired to northern Florida at his Suwannee River home and continues to distinguish himself in another area: oil painting, for which he has won several blue ribbons at north Florida art shows. Things are pretty much back to normal at St. Petersburg High School. Though there is a new science building and the science classes are no longer on the third floor or attic rooms, faculty still remember the teacher whose influence on Florida extends through some of its most prominent citizens. Some of the stories of his career, including the strange occurrences, have nearly been forgotten. These are the stories of a teacher whose influence on his students may have reached beyond the grave.

Skyway Bridge Hitchhiker

The Sunshine Skyway Bridge that connects Tampa and St. Petersburg is a magnificent structure that dominates the skyline and steals attention even from the nearby beaches. It has arched over numerous tragedies and has been the jumping-off point of a number of successful and unsuccessful suicide attempts.

The Skyway was built after the bridge over Tampa Bay became the scene of an accident in 1980 that brought down one of its sections, drivers and all, into Tampa Bay. The phosphate carrier *Summit Venture* was swept by a vicious squall into one of the bridge supports, collapsing a section of the bridge into Tampa Bay along with a number of cars and a Greyhound bus. Thirty-five people were killed. The old bridge was torn down except for its approaches, which were turned into fishing piers, and the new one was opened close by in 1987.

Whether daytime or darkness, the older, lower bridge was often shrouded in fog. It was a perfect modern-day setting for ghosts. At least some ghosts thought so.

The best known was the blonde. Once she was seen at the middle of the old bridge, as if she were going to jump. The other sightings of this woman were at one end of the bridge. She was described as young and attractive with blonde hair and blue eyes and wearing either a tight T-shirt or an off-white cotton outfit. She was hitchhiking but seemed to be afraid of something. Despite the fact that nearly all the sightings were on foggy nights or mornings, the details of her appearances were specific, for a number of motorists actually picked her up and gave her a ride. These included out-of-state drivers who were unlikely to be in on a local legend or joke.

She said repeatedly that she needed to get to the other side of the bridge, but that she was afraid of crossing it. A number of her bene-factors tried to allay her intense fear, to no avail. They didn't have long to do it—by the time the vehicle reached the middle of the bridge, she had vanished.

The hitchhiker, not seen since 1980, is thought to be the spirit of one of the many people who committed suicide by jumping from the old bridge.

There are occasionally problems with motorists who stop at the middle of the newer Sunshine Skyway to gawk or take pictures; stopping is forbidden, but the view is spectacular. The view below must be terrifying, however, to someone who is plunging toward it in free fall and is already regretting the decision to jump.

If the phantom girl is still about, she's on a phantom bridge. Maybe she was able to follow the terrified victims of the 1980 disaster to wherever they went. Or since she never made it to the other side of the old bridge, could she have been a pre-1980 harbinger of the terror to come?

Spook Hill

A visit to Spook Hill in Lake Wales may prompt anything from an inquiry into ancient Seminole legend to a pit stop at one's automobile service shop. Either extreme will probably help one learn something, and the experience of Spook Hill itself will be worth talking (or writing) about.

The Seminoles were the first to see Spook Hill, but their reac-tions to it are unknown. They were mainly interested in establish-ing a campsite at nearby Lake Wailes (the town's name is spelled "Lake Wales" to distinguish it from the lake itself). This campsite would give them a high vantage point that was close to a place sacred to their sun god, as well as fresh water and good fishing. The Seminoles' presence made for good hunting, unfortunately, in the opinion of a huge bull alligator that eventually moved into the lake.

The alligator raided the village nightly. The animal proved too difficult to capture or kill, and soon the whole village lived in terror of sundown. Cufcowellax, the chief, realized that the alligator was more than just an overgrown lizard and set out to drive off or destroy this supernatural creature. He submitted to the ceremonies of the tribe's religious leaders and was placed under the protection of the Great Spirit.

Day after day the alligator hid deep within the lake. Night after night it used the shield of darkness to evade its sworn enemy. Finally the alligator was dragging yet another victim into the water at the northwest shore when it was surprised by daybreak and an angry chief. A long battle ensued on both land and water, lasting long enough on land to create a bowl-shaped depression in the ground nearby and furiously enough in the water to spill water from Lake Wailes into the depression, creating a smaller lake. Then the thrashing in the water stopped. The water turned red and calm.

A lone figure rose from the bloodied water. It was Cufcowellax. He was received with joy and much celebration. Much later, Cufcowellax died peacefully and was buried on the shore of the smaller lake, Lake Ticowa.

The Seminoles later moved farther south as the whites' settlements grew closer. The town of Lake Wales was established. The circuit riders who formed Florida's Pony Express and carried mail from one side of the peninsula to the other used the Seminole trail around Lake Ticowa. Having had to climb uphill as they approached the Lake Wales area, they were relieved to see the beginning of a downhill and then astounded to see that their horses were struggling to run down the slope.

The Seminoles had held the area of Lake Ticowa to be sacred, since it was the burial ground of a great chief who had bested an evil enemy with the help of the Great Spirit. The story was that the horses were being pulled back or resisted by either Cufcowellax or the bull alligator. Whatever the explanation, the circuit riders spread the word among their comrades about the strange place they called Spook Hill.

Lake Wales proved to be good citrus country, and the mules pulling the wagons around the lake got plenty of exercise trying to drag their loads down Spook Hill. Later the road was paved and a

Spook Hill, where cars roll apparently uphill
from the white line in the foreground

school was built across the road from the lake. Children struggling to get their bicycles uphill as they approach Spook Hill Elementary School find that they have to save some extra breath for the more demanding downhill journey.

I tested Spook Hill while the road was deserted on a weekend day, using a low-mileage, 1998, four-door Saturn. The road is two lanes and paved. It runs north and south, and it's best to be driving north on it. Signs tell about the phenomenon and some of its history. They also instruct vehicles to stop at a clearly seen white line on the road and to put the gears into neutral. It's a good idea to watch

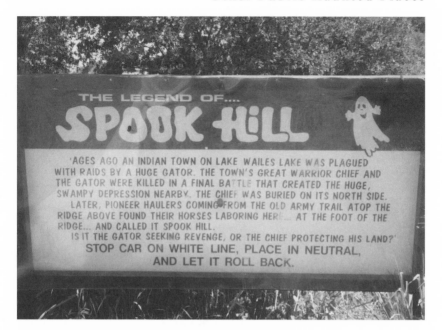

THE LEGEND OF....

SPOOK HiLL

'AGES AGO AN INDIAN TOWN ON LAKE WAILES LAKE WAS PLAGUED
WITH RAIDS BY A HUGE GATOR. THE TOWN'S GREAT WARRIOR CHIEF AND
THE GATOR WERE KILLED IN A FINAL BATTLE THAT CREATED THE HUGE,
SWAMPY DEPRESSION NEARBY. THE CHIEF WAS BURIED ON ITS NORTH SIDE.
LATER, PIONEER HAULERS COMING FROM THE OLD ARMY TRAIL ATOP THE
RIDGE ABOVE FOUND THEIR HORSES LABORING HERE... AT THE FOOT OF THE
RIDGE... AND CALLED IT SPOOK HILL.
IS IT THE GATOR SEEKING REVENGE, OR THE CHIEF PROTECTING HIS LAND?'
STOP CAR ON WHITE LINE, PLACE IN NEUTRAL,
AND LET IT ROLL BACK.

Explanatory sign at Spook Hill

for what's behind you as well as what's in front. The hill north of the white line seems to angle upward sharply, and the hill in the rearview mirror appears to slope upward a little more gently.

Placing the car in neutral and letting go of the brake, I remembered that some vehicles had been reported to roll uphill at least a few inches. My Saturn rolled backward (and apparently uphill) about *sixty feet*. I weigh about two hundred pounds and was alone in the car. I tried it again and went about the same distance.

There was still no one else around. I parked the car at the white line and stood by it, looking about carefully. The ground north of the white line appeared to slope downward for a short distance before the abruptly angled climb upwards. The ground south of the line and under the car looked like a gentle uphill before getting steeper. It appears that any car in neutral should roll forward (north) for about fifteen feet and then stop.

I got back into the car and drove around the block, this time stopping about a hundred feet from the white line, turning off the engine, putting the car into neutral, and releasing the brake. The car rolled forward all the way to the white line, but distinctly slowed down about twenty feet from it, as if the gentle slope south of the line was actually a gentle uphill. By this time I was on a roll, so I stayed at the white line for a moment with my brake on and then released the brake. This time I rolled backwards even farther, about seventy feet.

The Saturn has had routine maintenance service a number of times since then. No one has reported teeth marks on the bumper, so I doubt that Lake Wales is having any problems with phantom giant bull alligators. I did ask Ken at the service department why the car had rolled so far. He reminded me of the low mileage at the time and said that as cars get more mileage, the rear brake pad tends to pull away from the drum somewhat and cause friction with the tires. Newer cars will therefore roll farther with momentum than older ones, unless the brakes have just been serviced.

So if your car rolls only a short distance on Spook Hill, either the spirits or your brakes might be wearing out. Or maybe the grades are wearing down. I suppose that I could return with a carpenter's level and see what is uphill and what is an optical illusion. However, whatever force is capable of moving a Saturn uphill can push the bubble in a carpenter's level anywhere it wants.

In the meantime, I have added the job of teacher at Spook Hill Elementary to my list of jobs I don't want. They might make me teach science. And who would want to have to explain gravity to children who have spent their lunch hour watching their skateboards roll uphill?

Jessie May

If the May-Stringer House was in disrepair, neglected, and brooding at the top of a barren hill, there would be no question that it's being haunted. Instead the house is still being lovingly restored. It graces a small corner lot in Brooksville, reached from I-75 by a quiet drive through the countryside of Hernando County. The lot is grassy and flat. Near the house is a small gazebo. Behind it is a well-tended memorial garden. Inside it is Jessie May. At three years of

May-Stringer House

age, she is the youngest volunteer in the Hernando County Historical Society. She is likely to retain that distinction. She has been three for over a hundred years now. She doesn't show her age. She doesn't even show. But like other playful and mischievous little girls, there is no mistaking her tracks.

The director of the historical society, Ms. Virginia Jackson, was gracious enough to open the house for me on a day when it was normally closed. We met while rushing about; as I had pulled up to the house, a gust of wind blew papers from a table on the porch. We gathered them up together and then introduced ourselves.

The house is not one to rush into. It is light and cheery inside, but from the first step, the restoration's attention to detail is obvious. Light-colored wallpaper keeps the walls from closing in. The hardwood floors creak slightly as we walk about. Crystal decorations tinkle from my footfalls. Air conditioning has banished the mustiness of aged homes.

Near a fireplace is a table on which is displayed a tea set. There are settings for two. "Some time ago, one of our volunteers accidentally broke one of the cups," related Ms. Jackson. "We took away the rest of the setting and left one on the table. We have several other settings stored away in the next room. We closed up and went home for the night. The next morning we came in and found two complete settings on the table. None of us had done it, and no one else could have. We figured that Jessie May didn't want a tea party for one," she laughed. "Sometimes we find a third setting laid out as well."

Two old photographs are on the right as one enters the next room. The top one is of John Saxon, the father of Jessie May Saxon. The lower one is of Jessie May herself as an infant of three or four months. She is asleep in her crib. Her face looks remarkably like that of one of my daughters at that age. Later I would find that both she and that particular daughter were born on the same date: February 19. It is the date when Jessie's mother died giving birth to her.

A newspaper account reports that Jessie's voice can be heard at times crying, "Mama, Mama," as she searches for her lost mother. Jessie herself died at age three. Some say that she missed her mother so much that she died of a broken heart.

That has not been Ms. Jackson's experience. "I was vacuuming in the attic one day while alone in the house. To reach certain spots, I had to unplug the vacuum and use another socket. Whenever I stopped vacuuming, I could hear something in the attic. It was soft and sounded like a little girl crying from fear. I couldn't make out any words, certainly not 'Mama.' I could hear it only for a few minutes at a time. It was coming from one side of the attic, but I couldn't see anyone there. Then I would start vacuuming again, and the crying would be there when I stopped.

"Three workmen have heard her crying while they were doing restoration or repairs in other parts of the house. Two of them will not come inside anymore. The third one told me that he was cutting some wood with an electric saw. Whenever he stopped, he could hear the same frightened voice that I did. He thinks it was Jessie May.

"I don't understand why I would be hearing her in the attic. There was no attic when she was living in this house."

We found out later that afternoon.

In front of another fireplace are a number of simple wooden toys from times past. They are not placed in any order. It would do no good to do so; frequently the staff enters the house to find that the toys have been moved about since the day before. One or two may even be in another room. Over eight thousand articles from the past are exhibited within the museum. One is a set of baby shoes that often and inexplicably appear prominently displayed on a certain chair. Another large group is from the practice of yesteryear's medicine. Part of the house had been used as a medical office, and there is a fascinating collection of the tools of the healing arts in that part of the house.

If Jessie May had been following us to hear more about herself, she must have spent at least twenty minutes impatiently rolling her eyes and keeping her hands on her invisible hips as I poked about. I hope that she enjoyed hearing the stories and anecdotes that Ms. Jackson had retrieved from the past as much as I did.

At the top of the stairs leading to the second floor is a small play area for Jessie May. Toys, a dollhouse, and a child's furniture are placed in front of a closet whose door is sealed shut. It is thought that Jessie May used the closet when she was alive. Naturally, the play area is frequently rearranged at night when no one is there. Lights come on in the house after having been turned off for the night, long after people have locked up and gone home.

"She can't possibly resist this," I commented when I saw the full-sized replica of a schoolroom on the second floor. Ms. Jackson agreed. She recounted how often the volunteer in charge of that area has to inspect the room and put everything back into place before opening to the public that day. Jessie May likes the marbles best.

We climbed the stairs to the attic. Ms. Jackson showed me the part of the attic that the voice had come from. There was nothing unusual looking about it.

"Take a look at this. We found it when we moved some furniture a little while ago." We stepped past a couple of couches and a twin bed. Near the end of the attic was an opening in the floor just large enough for an adult to go through. It was the top of a hidden stairway, leading from the sealed closet on the second floor. The shape of the attic around the opening would have reflected any sound from the closet area throughout the attic. If Jessie was the source of the mysterious sounds in the attic, she didn't have to be in there to be making herself heard.

We finished the visit in the office, where Ms. Jackson kindly offered to photocopy the pictures of Jessie May and of her father for me, since I had been so interested in them. At that point, Jessie May may have gotten her revenge for my ignoring her while studying the medical exhibit. The copies of her picture came out fine. Her father's picture wouldn't print at all. All we got were two black sheets of paper. The photo had been copied earlier with no trouble on another machine in the house, so Ms. Jackson tried on that one.

In the moments while she was away, I looked around the office and the small gift shop. Research of the past is important at the museum. Papers, booklets, and pamphlets are filed and ready for filing. Like an array of freshly cut jewels from a mine, booklets on various facets of Hernando County history are neatly arranged on one wall. The material in the booklets shows a different past than present-day hearsay and legends depict. The booklets are not only more accurate, they are more interesting. They tell stories like that of the successful and hard-working Hernando County farmer who joined the Union Army during the Civil War. To keep the county from supplying food to the Rebels, he returned with other Union sympathizers and destroyed his own farm.

"I'm sorry. I've copied this picture before. This is very strange," said a somewhat flustered Ms. Jackson as she reappeared with another black sheet of paper. I suggested we give up. We were wasting a lot of toner.

I wondered aloud how Jessie May had died.

"There was a lot of diphtheria and yellow fever in Hernando County in those days. It might have been one of those diseases that took her away."

Yellow fever is bad enough. I hoped it wasn't diphtheria.

"A little while ago we were doing some research and looked at all the headstones in the cemeteries here in the county," she continued. "It is sad. Most of the ones from that time are those of children." There were generations of grief in her voice. She noted that Jessie May's gravesite location was not known. Neither was that of her brother, who only lived a month after delivery.

I thanked Ms. Jackson and left with what I had: a brochure on the May-Stringer House, my notes, two copies of the picture of Jessie May, and three black sheets of failed attempts to get a picture of anyone else…something else to credit to a mischievous little girl.

Time herds us along a path in one direction only. Perhaps some of us have somehow been a part of Jessie May's dreams. Somewhere off that path, she may still be dreaming of a time when mothers hardly ever die in childbirth. In her dreams, she may hear a loud, high-pitched whining noise and it frightens her because it comes from above or outside and it reminds her of the fierce winds of a tornado or hurricane. I do not know what would happen if one warned her that there was going to be a noise before the vacuum cleaner was turned on. It does interest me that only the toys and objects from her time period are played with.

The museum is not a bad place to be in one's dreams. It is a place where the lessons of the past are carefully preserved. And what motherless child would not want to be in a place where children are welcomed and cherished?

Still Serving

Military Ghosts

The Phantom Civil War Patrol

One of the strangest sightings of ghosts in Florida occurs in the Panhandle, northeast of Pensacola. Hunters have seen a Confederate patrol led by a "gimlet-eyed officer" at nighttime, moving stealthily across a curve of the Yellow River. It is difficult to ascertain what the soldiers are doing in that area near Crestview, roughly fifty miles east-northeast of Pensacola in Okaloosa County. A little farther north is the Alabama state line.

History doesn't help much. Skirmishes did happen between small bands of Union and Confederate soldiers as the Yanks strayed from their ships blockading the Pensacola area in search of food. The problem with depriving the Confederates of food transportation was that the pickings were slim for the Union as well. As the Union soldiers prowled the farms and fields, they were tracked by the Confederates and sometimes attacked by them. The Old Bethel Cemetery near Crestview contains some unmarked Union graves.

There is an old tree near the Yellow River that used to be in the middle of the Blackwater River before that river changed its course and meandered farther west. On the tree are carved the initials "CSA," an arrow pointing southeast, a gun, a spur, and a rowel. There is nothing southeast now except Eglin Air Force Base. The Yellow and Blackwater Rivers course southwest, not southeast, as they empty into the bay east of Pensacola.

No one knows what the patrol was doing out there in the dark of night. Unfortunately, the nature of war is such that the members of the patrol and their leader may not have known either. A more supernatural explanation could be that someone or something misled the patrol into this wild area, where they perished, but no Union operatives claimed responsibility for the carvings. Perhaps a dead Union soldier had taken the opportunity to revenge himself on the CSA by carving the strange and misleading trail sign.

The Phantoms of Fort Taylor

Fort Zachary Taylor is not at the end of the earth, but it is at one end of the United States. It occupies the southwest corner of Key West. Start in Maine at the Canadian border and drive down I-95 to Miami, and then access the bridge that connects the Florida Keys to the mainland. Keep going all the way to Key West. Park when you can drive no farther, and walk through the fort until you run out of continental United States and find yourself in water.

It's a relatively easy drive back to the mainland and family. It was not so for those who served there in bygone days, when Key West was accessible only by boat. There were no airlifts or quick-response elite military units. Some military people served their terms of duty and left. Some never left. Others are still serving.

One historian was searching through the fort for some of the big guns thought to be buried there. Things weren't going well, even though there were only so many places on an island that cannons could be hidden. One night he awoke to find a cheerful apparition in Confederate uniform staring at him. The apparition told him where to find one of the big guns. The gun was found at that precise spot. The apparition appeared again later and identified itself as Wendell Gardiner. Later, a tourist remarked offhandedly to the researcher that an ancestor of his, Wendell Gardiner, had served at the fort.

When the tourists have left and the rangers have closed the fort for the night, Wendell is not alone. Whistling and howls are heard at night, and even "Dixie" can be heard being sung. Voices are heard from empty places, perhaps from times past.

Spectral soldiers are seen, then vanish. One was observed walking through a wall. Shafts of light through empty corridors are broken by shadows cast by something unseen. The soldiers are most often noted as the sun sets, or in the early morning hours. Each day the park rangers go to the office to see which objects have been moved about the night before.

Around Halloween, it's possible to catch a ghostly tour of Fort Taylor, but it is not a spectral freak show. The staff is quick to remind visitors that these ghosts are reminders of a time when devotion to duty and country was taken seriously, even by civilians. Unlike most other spooks one might encounter, the most appropriate reaction to a ghost encountered at Fort Taylor might be a salute.

A Confederate Funeral

In March of 1998, a funeral procession arrived in Florida over a hundred years late. The remains of a Confederate soldier who had died while walking back home from the war were found in South Carolina, considerably northeast of where his family lived in Plant City. Once his grave was located, his remains were brought back to Florida in a formal ceremony that brought the world of the mid-1800s across the hubbub of the 1990s. Cars stopped and wondered as the procession crossed busy interstates on its way to Plant City. Sponsored in part by the United Daughters of the Confederacy, the ceremony brought a little more closure to a part of Florida history.

Was it all worth it? It was for the person who told me the story. It is hard to say whether funerals are truly for the living or for the dead. In the aftermath of the burial, the question rose anew. Among the many photographs taken of the event, three different photographers who used different cameras and had their film developed in different places found the apparition of a Confederate soldier standing next to the coffin before it was lowered into the new gravesite.

Fort Clinch

Standing within Fort Clinch, located in the state park of the same name, one would initially think it would be a paradise of a duty station. Situated along part of the beachfront of Florida's northernmost barrier island, the fort is close to everything that Amelia Island can offer. Within the fort, however, careful preservation and living history volunteers reveal the real hardships that made military service there a true service and not a vacation. The volunteers act as if they really are living in the 1800s. So do the ghosts.

One volunteer who was asleep in his bunk one night was awakened by the unmistakable sound of boots clomping up to his side. When he turned to see who was waking him, no one was there. Volunteers at the fort hospital have seen an extra member of their staff—a woman in white like a nurse, carrying a lantern.

A remarkable aspect of the Fort Clinch stories is the amount of interaction between the ranger staff, the volunteers, and the ghosts. Some members of a volunteer encampment one weekend, during a July full moon, saw four spectral soldiers in Confederate uniforms marching across the parade grounds, up the ramp, and over the wall.

The same volunteers made certain they were at the fort the following year during the July full moon. This time, only three of the soldiers came marching across the parade grounds. As they marched upon the ramp, one of the onlookers called out and asked where the fourth man was.

"He's sick tonight. Couldn't come," was the answer.

Another volunteer was staying on the top floor of one of the storehouses. While the volunteer was looking for something and having some difficulty because of the dark, a woman walked by with a lantern. On request, the woman stayed and held the lantern aloft till the item was found. She then left the room. The volunteer tried to find and thank her later that evening, but the woman was nowhere to be found, and no one else had seen her.

The Living History garrisons are held the first weekend of each month and at other special times of the year. A candlelight tour is also offered. The quality of the Living History presentation is high. In fact, one may never know at times whether one is witnessing a historical reenactment or a haunting.

Magnolia Hall

It was nightfall at Magnolia Hall in Apalachicola. From the places in the brush where they concealed themselves, the Confederate soldiers in the area used the remaining light to search the house's roof. A nail keg on the roof meant that Union soldiers were about.

There was no telling where Yanks might come from. They had already damaged the lighthouse just south on St. George Island. Farther southeast and across the open Gulf, one Hernando County farmer who sympathized with the Union had returned to his farm in uniform from his Union unit. He destroyed it, despite his years of hard work on the land, to keep the Rebels from getting any food from his property.

There had been no Union uniforms seen at Apalachicola for a long time now. People still looked upward to the top of the house for a nail keg. Many hopes and fears were focused there.

Sadie Orman knew that the boys in gray uniforms needed all the help they could get. With their backs against the Gulf, they were miles and years from their homes. She was lucky enough to be in her household. They had left theirs, or been driven from them, to serve a cause that they and she believed in. Some of the Confederates had heard of the war reaching their hometowns. They knew that they had nowhere else to go but here.

Once again this evening, there was no nail keg in sight. Young soldiers in the familiar gray garb moved quietly through the grounds around the house. They could be seen in the moonlight by any locals who were around, but the locals had long ago learned to avoid the place because of the Confederate guards. The soldiers were armed but stealthy. They cloaked themselves in silence. If they whispered among themselves, no one else heard them. No twigs broke. They stepped softly through the grass as they watched over the household that watched over them.

There were lights going on inside the house, but none of the young men peeked inside—that would be disrespectful to Mrs. Orman or whoever else was within. If the young men had looked, they might have seen a calendar or a newspaper, on which the year was clearly written.

It was the year 2000.

The spirits of what used to be the Orman-Butterfield house have never bothered the present owners. When I spoke with Douglas Gaidry, he said that the only possible encounter he had had was one night soon after he and his wife, Anna, had bought the house. "At one o'clock in the morning," he recalled, "I heard a door slam. I got up and checked all over the house and all the doors were closed. So I went back to bed. At two o'clock I heard another door slam. I didn't know what to make of it. The next day I noticed a screen door that might have come loose in the wind. That's the closest encounter I've had, if there was one.

"This house will soon be taken over by the state as a historic site. We've enjoyed living here. When we had it as a bed-and-breakfast, no one ever had a bad experience. Sometimes people would tell us that they had heard or seen something they thought was strange. Some would ask if the place was haunted, and of course we'd tell them the stories we had heard. We charged a lot for our rooms. By and large, the people who came were intelligent people who could afford to pay a lot. Many are still our good friends. But some of them definitely saw something."

The previous family in the house had had a number of encounters, Mr. Gaidry continued. "One of the daughters has a husband who came over once to fix the water heater. After he was done he went upstairs to lie down for a bit. He heard the doorknob turning. He looked up and saw the doorknob turn. Then the door opened but

Magnolia Hall

no one was there. He jumped up from the bed and ran to the door, but the hallway was empty and there were no footsteps. He went all over the house and looked outside too but couldn't find anyone. He didn't go back.

"I met him later. He owns a shop in town and does well; he is well thought of. I introduced myself and said that I had heard the story about him. He told me everything he remembered and assured me that every bit was true."

It seemed that in the earlier days of the house, the ghosts had more trouble from the living than the other way around. Mrs. Gaidry related, "One daughter had a friend spend the night who was a Jehovah's Witness. The next morning the friend decided to get rid of the ghost…with an exorcism, I think. She went upstairs and when she came down, she was shaking. She put her little book down and ran out. She never came back.

"Another friend came over once who was a big burly fellow. He said he didn't believe in ghosts and that he certainly wasn't afraid of them. He went charging up the stairs and never got to the top—some kind of force pushed him back down."

One of the few actual sightings of a ghost inside the house was by the wife of a painter. She was staying in one of the rooms while her husband did some repainting of the house. As she approached her room one day, she saw the white form of a woman in the doorway to the room. She rushed into the room, which had no other doors, but no one was there.

And what of the spectral Confederate guards outside? The Gaidrys have yet to see them, but they often hear from neighbors who have definitely seen them. Some who live nearby will not go near the house at night because of what they have seen. The only clue has been a peculiar odor within the house, which they smell occasionally but cannot associate with any definite weather condition or wind direction. It's the odor of gunpowder.

The young men in their gray Confederate uniforms step softly through the grass, guarding the house that watches over them. Their youth and their innocence have been left behind on the first battlefield. The lucky ones are years and miles from their homes. Others have learned that the war has left no homes for them to return to. What kept them going, and what keeps them going still? Their cause has long passed from fashion and favor. Perhaps they understand better than most what so many people today have forgotten: how much Sadie Orman risked in order to help them.

If Sadie had been caught by Union soldiers, the keg of nails might have been all that was left once they burned her house to the ground. In those days, there was no 9-1-1 to call, no television crews to appeal to the communities for help, no airplanes to fly to the homes of relatives, and no way for a president to drop in for a day. A Confederate widow who had lost her home in a hostile land could expect little relief as she waited for the carpetbaggers to pick her clean.

There are some who insist that Sadie Orman is still in the house she loved so dearly but was willing to risk. Others have seen the boys in gray who stand watch around her, bound willingly to the house for over a century by duty, gratitude, and honor.

Far away, and down on the peninsula of Florida, a retired military pilot and his wife bow their heads over their evening meal. I know them and know how badly they were treated by the company that built their house. I would have been bitter. They aren't, for they know that they would then lose the sense of gratitude that has always been important to them. They have lived long enough to know what to nurture within their hearts and what to starve out. To those of us who are still too young to understand the power of gratitude, the old military couple and the spirits of Apalachicola have much to teach.

At Least They Wear the Sheets Instead of Stealing Them:

The Haunting of Hotels

Biltmore Hotel

It has been called the largest haunted house in the world and the most haunted hotel in Florida. When it was empty, locals used to gather on its golf course to watch lights within the building that were not supposed to be there.

The Biltmore Hotel has a long and colorful history. Even during a period of years when it was not open for business, its history was growing. A group of science fiction enthusiasts once explored its vacant halls and rooms with a tape recorder; nothing out of the ordinary was heard. However, when they returned home and played the tape, there was the sound of heavy breathing and of a sigh that had not been heard in the hotel itself.

Another tape was made during a séance in the hotel. In the midst of the séance, one psychic was disturbed because she sensed

The Biltmore

a little old man with a cane. No one else sensed him, but the tape later played a tapping sound that had not been heard before.

The Biltmore Hotel is thriving now. So are the spirits. Messages may be found written on steamy mirrors, lampshades disappear, and waitresses carrying trays find doors being opened for them by unseen hands. Some think that the Biltmore has more ghosts than guests. Whatever the true number, none of them act malevolently. Considering the history of one of them, the atmosphere of supernaturally good cheer is surprising.

Thomas "Fatty" Walsh was a gangster who had moved to Miami from New York, partly to escape bothersome inquiries from the local police about some bodies that had recently turned up. This was during Prohibition, and he found a convenient business partnership with a friend who was renting the thirteenth and fourteenth floors of the Biltmore. Illegal liquor and gambling comprised the business on these floors, and the patrons were some of Miami's finest.

All went well for Mr. Walsh till he and his partner argued one night, and Walsh was shot on the thirteenth floor. The access routes to the floors from below had been blocked, so the police were not able to get to the scene until the patrons, the gambling parapher-nalia, and all the bottles of booze had been moved safely elsewhere. Nothing was found except Walsh's body and an injured friend who had tried to intervene. The friend wasn't talking.

Paranormal activity is not confined to the thirteenth floor, but most of it is there. Baggage carts wheel down the hall by themselves. Some think that Walsh gets lonely up there and just wants compa-ny. Elevators stop on the thirteenth floor even though that button hasn't been pushed. Those who come to look around the thirteenth floor and then prepare to leave sometimes hear a baby's cry, tempt-ing them to stay longer and search the area. Room service employ-ees find the floor curiously convenient, for when their hands are full, there are never any objects in the way or doors that need open-ing.

Pranks, such as a "Boo!" written on a steamed bathroom mirror, are good natured and gentle. Whatever his past, "Fatty" Walsh has retained a mischievous sense of humor and a unique form of gang-ster gallantry.

Boca Raton Resort and Club

In Boca Raton, only the unreal may be real. A walk through its decades shows a panorama of once-in-a-lifetime sights: visiting royalty, electrically powered Italian gondolas for a nonexistent canal, the most famous Hollywood stars of their day, and a three-hundred-pound ex-Californian lumbering through a world-famous hotel in silk pajamas with a macaw on his shoulder and two large monkeys dutifully following him.

The planning of Boca Raton seems to have left out the hum-drum. The world's standards were merely starting points for what Boca Raton was planned to become. The ordinary, day-to-day plod

Boca Raton Resort and Club
Photograph used by permission of Boca Raton Resort and Club

of normal life appears to have been squeezed out of existence by grandeur, lavishness, wealth, flamboyance, and architectural brilliance. The humdrum has taken refuge mostly in the spiritual side of life, where it can keep discreetly out of sight.

The ordinary can be found in Boca Raton, sort of. Its tracks can be seen in the least likely of places—the third-floor Cloister Hallway of the Boca Raton Resort and Club. The tracks are of Esmeralda. She is a ghost. She bothers no one. Her footsteps have been heard on the third floor. She moves from room to room. No one sees her, but they see the lights turned off that have been carelessly left on. Objects have been moved but only back into their proper places.

It is not known for certain who Esmeralda was when she was mortal. Some think that when famed architect Addison Mizner opened the Cloisters in 1926, she was one of the first chambermaids hired. She probably worked quietly as some of the wealthiest people in the world walked by her. She may have winced as Mizner himself strolled the halls in his silk pajamas, with his animals on his shoulders and in his shadow.

No matter how famous or eccentric the occupants were, lights were still carelessly left on or off, and rooms needed to be tidied. The land-boom times that had helped give birth to the Cloisters came and went. Ownerships changed, and new openings were accompanied by new additions of services and buildings for the pampering of guests. Through it all, there was always Esmeralda to tend to what we take for granted. At some point she may have died, but death is only an inconvenience to those people with the spirit of Boca Raton. It is a place powered by dreams. By their nature, dreams do not include the inconveniences of reality. So Esmeralda goes on showing up for work as expected, handling the mundane business of everyday life on behalf of others. At least on her shift and on her floor.

Casablanca Inn

The Casablanca Inn is now a bed-and-breakfast, one of the most popular ones in St. Augustine. The inn has a long list of charms and superlatives, one of which is its view of Matanzas Bay. Its place in history, however, has more to do with the bay's view of the inn.

When the Volstead Act banned the manufacture and sale of alcohol throughout the United States in 1919, the inn was known as the Matanzas Hotel. The widow (whose name will be withheld to protect the guilty) who owned the elegant hotel kept it clean, comfortable, and reasonably priced. The food was both delicious and plentiful. The hotel was well known throughout its region to all who appreciated the best, including the rumrunners who transport-ed illegal liquor from Cuba and other Caribbean islands to the Atlantic coast. A spirited business relationship soon developed between the well-bred but enterprising proprietress and the rum-runners.

Boatloads of liquor were brought into St. Augustine in the ensu-ing years. Guests and locals who were "in the know" could come to the hotel for a few days at a time and get their share of the Cuban and Jamaican imports. Then the shop would temporarily close as the rumrunners moved farther up the coast.

Treasury agents were assigned to look for violators of Prohibition throughout the United States. There were not enough agents to handle all the illicit activity along Florida's Atlantic coast, but even-tually a few of them came to the hotel and began inquiring. By this time the widow had become romantically involved with one of the rumrunners. She said she had no information for the Treasury agents.

The T-men liked what they saw. The place was well run, and the rates were within the reach of their modest budgets. As they worked their way up and down the coast from Daytona Beach to Jacksonville, they called ahead for reservations whenever they planned to stay in St. Augustine. The crafty owner realized that she alone knew when the T-men would be in town and when it was safe for her other clients to pursue their business.

She worked out a simple system. The boats from the Caribbean would pause at night a couple of miles from St. Augustine at one of the many places from which the hotel could be seen. If there were no T-men in town, she would wave a lantern several times from the widow's walk on the roof of the building. If government agents lurked downstairs, she stayed downstairs with them.

The rumrunners paid her well for her information. By the time Prohibition was repealed in 1933, she was a millionaire. Later she died and was buried in Huguenot Cemetery, something that one of the cemetery's former residents may still be unhappy about. (See Chapter 3, "There Goes the Neighborhood.")

Guests at an adjacent inn have had good reason to wonder whether her story is still going on. There have been numerous incidents of a bright light shining through their windows at nighttime — light that is thought to be from the lighthouse on Anastasia Island. Upon looking into the matter though, investigators have found that the light has clearly been coming from the roof of the Casablanca, although no lights up there are capable of that kind of brilliance. Shrimpers and fishermen entering the bay on a moonless night have gotten used to seeing the phantom lantern waving from the roof of the Casablanca, guiding them safely in. Some have even seen a dark figure holding and waving the light.

Inside the recently renovated Casablanca Inn itself, the benign and spectral figure of an elderly woman has been seen. Objects that have been mislaid show up in unlikely but obvious places, as if they have been found and returned to their owners. And one photograph taken recently shows a female apparition, perhaps still waiting for her Caribbean lover's return.

Cassadaga's Haunted Hotel

Any settlement that has been founded and run by spiritualists would be expected to have a significant proportion of its population that can neither be seen nor heard. Fortunately, the voting requirements are too stringent to include residents of the noncorporeal persuasion.

The hotel there is haunted, as one would expect. Arthur was an Irish tenor who particularly liked the area and stayed in room 22. It is also where he died. The room has sometimes been reported to smell of cigars, gin, or pine needles. Gin smells somewhat like pine needles, and Arthur liked cigars. Even body odor has been noted in the room — Arthur lived before air conditioning, and Cassadaga's heat and humidity can be intense. A chair in the hotel has been seen to rock by itself.

Arthur has been seen in hallways. People have attempted to contact him, and it is claimed that he will turn lights on and off in response to questions. He is also playful—one guest complained of being repeatedly pushed out of bed.

Strange music, like vintage music being played too fast from a distance, has been heard by guests in room 22, though no one else was staying on the floor and televisions and radios are not allowed in the rooms. A muffled scream was also heard. Is Arthur playing pranks and entertaining guests who expect a spooky show?

Herlong Mansion

Twelve miles south of Gainesville is the charming home of eight hundred souls named Micanopy. Inside Micanopy is the Herlong Mansion, the home of one spirit named Inez. She is like other spirits in Florida's bed-and-breakfasts in that she is harmless. She inhabits more than she haunts the place. As everything around her retains a seductive charm and the best of yesteryear, Inez herself has flirted with progress. She is a rare ghost: She has her own page on the World Wide Web.

Inez's journey to the Web began in the 1840s, when a small and simple house was built in what would become Micanopy. As 1900 approached, Inez was the first child born into her family in their home in South Carolina. The family was initially well-to-do, but their fortunes were reversing. Soon there were six children in the family. Inez's mother inherited the small house in Micanopy from a relative. Deciding that business would be better in Florida, they moved to Micanopy around 1910.

Packing the family of eight into the small house was not easy, and Inez's father quickly decided that the family had slid far enough toward bottom. Interests were begun in timber and citrus, both of which proved profitable. The small house was expanded into the mansion that today's guests now enjoy as one of Florida's best-known bed-and-breakfasts.

Inez married and moved out, but she fondly remembered the elegant and gracious life in the mansion. Her mother died later. She had retained title to the house. In her will, the house was divided equally among the children on the condition that their father be allowed to stay in it as long as he wished.

As it was, he wished to stay in it until he died, which was ten years later. Inez, already a widow, had now lost her mother and her father. She did not want to lose the house. Her late husband had left her and their children enough money to allow her to buy out her siblings and take the Herlong Mansion for herself. None of the other Herlong descendants had the resources to buy the house. The bitter two-year wrangling that followed cost Inez what was left of her birth family—no other Herlong ever entered the mansion again.

It turned out that Inez's siblings hadn't done much to maintain the house during the years after their mother had died. Once she took possession, Inez set about restoring her home. There was twelve years' worth of neglect to undo and a happier time to recover. She was working on the second floor in her estranged sister Mae's room when she died of a heart attack.

The mansion changed hands, and it was decided to make it a bed-and-breakfast. A group of workers from Wisconsin that specialized in restoration work was hired to finish the job that Inez had begun so well. With no electricity in the house, the men worked by daylight and slept on the parlor floor at night.

They slept for a few hours, anyway. They were the first to find that they had been told the truth and nothing but the truth about the house: that Inez had begun restoring it, that she had had a heart attack, and that she had died. It was a logical assumption to expect that Inez had left the house.

Then, as so often happens now, logic crumbles before experience.

The workers awoke after midnight to the sound of a second-floor door opening and closing. Footsteps came from the second-story hallway. Certain that whoever was making the noises had no honorable reason to be inside the house, the men went up the front stairway to confront the intruder. There was no one to be seen between them and the back stairway, and nothing to hear but their own breathing.

The second night of their stay, they awoke again to the sounds of the door opening and closing and footsteps in the hallway. Feeling surly, they rushed up the back stairs to face whoever had disrupted their sleep two nights in a row and to inquire as to his reasons for doing so. Again, there was nothing but empty hallway between them and the other stairway. The next step was obvious: two groups of men, one for each stairway, and a set of weapons for each group. The necessary items were procured the next day.

Anticipation probably came more easily than sleep that night. At the sound of the door, they exploded up both stairways only to face …each other. There was no other way out of the hallway. Whatever had been there was either invisible, could vanish at will, or could pass through solid objects such as walls. More importantly, it wasn't in their contract.

The fourth night, the good folks from Wisconsin slept peacefully in a motel at their employers' expense, having left the house as soon as darkness fell. Anxious to hold down expenses and to protect the reputation of the mansion, the owners locked themselves in a second-floor bedroom of the mansion and slept well that night. They awoke the next morning both refreshed and stunned to find the bedroom door unlocked and standing ajar.

Needless to say, the boys from Wisconsin got to stay in their cozy digs away from Inez while they finished their work. They're gone. The bed-and-breakfast is still there and doing a justifiably thriving business. At the Herlong Mansion itself, the owner spends many mornings inquiring of the guests as to how their night was. The guests then find out where Inez's room was and, on occasion, who among them had experienced a most elusive kind of Southern hospitality.

Seven Sisters Inn

I s there a ghost here?"…click…Silence, then a dial tone. Bonnie Morehardt turned to her husband, Ken Oden. "They hung up on us." It was obvious that they weren't going to learn anything from the previous owners. The two new owners of the Seven Sisters Inn in the historic district of Ocala were on their own with this one.

What had prompted the phone call was a presence that both of them had been sensing throughout the Queen Anne–style Victorian house, particularly on the third floor. There was no specific manifestation initially.

Bonnie recounted, "Both of us had 'feelings' about the third floor, which is an open loft that we'll be enclosing next year. The presence seemed much stronger when no guests were around. After a while I found myself talking to it when I was up there, reassuring it that we were there to take care of the house and to bring love into it."

As they spent the next several years refurbishing and remodeling the inn, they lived in a bedroom on the first floor. During that time they found themselves getting more and more interested in the history of the house and of Ocala itself. There seemed to be no other way to find an explanation for the odd events that began to occur.

"Light bulbs keep burning out, especially while I'm turning them on or off," Bonnie told me. "Sometimes I have to ask others to turn the lights on or off for me, because it happens more often when I do it, and it gets expensive. Candles get blown out. We had a wedding here once during which we wanted to have two candles burning. There was no draft in the room, and the air conditioning wasn't on, but the candles kept getting blown out. We lit them again and again until, in front of everyone, one candle flew across the room. Then we decided, 'Okay, no candles this time.' Then everything was fine."

Research has shown that the house was built in 1888 on a site involved in a huge fire two years before. More recently, before they had bought the house, it had been struck by lightning and a fire had resulted. Between the fire and the resulting water damage, the inn had been closed for five months. Perhaps the resident spirit wasn't taking chances on any more fires.

The "presence" continued to be sensed by the couple. Bonnie thought it was male. Her impression was stronger when a workman who had been doing some remodeling on the second floor came down and asked if they had seen the hammer he had borrowed. No one knew what he was talking about. He explained that the other workman, an older man in old-style clothing, had loaned him a hammer. When he had finished hammering, he put the hammer down. Now he could find neither the hammer nor the other workman.

As it happened, there was supposed to be only one workman in the house that day. No one else knew of a second, but men who were helping with the remodeling of the inn saw the phantom on two other occasions. As Bonnie and Ken had sensed, he was never frightening. If anything, their ghost was proving to be helpful, though overly cautious when it came to candles and other lights. A small table showed that their guest was also a bit of a klutz.

"We had a reading table on the third floor next to a window. One can step through the window onto a small part of the roof," explained Bonnie. "The table seemed to be in something's way. We would be downstairs and hear the table fall over. We would go up and check and, sure enough, it was on its side or even upside down. Three times it was broken in half. We finally moved it downstairs into a first floor bedroom, and it's just fine there."

I asked whether it might have been a pet jumping onto the table.

"The cat won't go up there. Sometimes I'll be carrying her with me when I go upstairs to turn out the lights, and she tries to get out of my arms on the way up. We often hear noises from upstairs when no guests are there, such as furniture being bumped, footsteps, and doors closing."

Despite a touch of clumsiness, the ghost has good reflexes. "A friend of mine, Yolanda, used to work here. She was carrying a load of towels up the stairs. Near the top, she lost her balance and fell backwards. She thought I had caught her from the back and put her back on her feet. When she turned around, no one was there. I was in another room downstairs at the time."

Soon there were signs that there was a feminine spirit in the inn as well. Each of the guest rooms had a book for the visitors to write in. At least two sets of visitors recorded that upon going to bed, their hair was gently brushed out of their faces or that they were tucked in by something unseen. Bonnie and Ken named the female spirit "Judy," and the bedroom where she seemed most to manifest herself they called "Judy's room."

"A couple who were staying in Judy's room came up to us one morning and asked if there were a spirit there. The husband had been waiting in the room while his wife was putting on her make-up at one of the sinks. She looked into the mirror and saw a woman standing behind her, also looking into the mirror. The entire form was white, and there was an outline of a face. As soon as she called out to her husband, the spirit turned and walked out of the room, right past him. He saw her too."

It was getting to where Bonnie and Ken might have to start paying as guests and staying at their own inn just to get in on the fun, but finally Bonnie saw a spirit for herself.

Bonnie reported, "I was standing with some other people in the dining room, and something caught my eye. I looked down the hall, and there she was! It was a woman like the one the people in Judy's room had seen. It was a white figure of a woman, with dark hair pulled back and wearing a long gray skirt that reached to the floor. She had as well a long-sleeved white blouse on that had a high neck. There was an aura around her. I saw her walking, not floating, across the hall from the kitchen and right through the wall into the back bedroom. That back bedroom used to be the kitchen. She didn't look at me. She was looking straight ahead."

Bonnie was glad she had finally seen one of the spirits and asked others about it. "I talked to a man who had owned the building about thirty years before, and he had seen her too.

"At first we were uneasy because of the presence we kept feeling when we bought the place. What really made a difference was when I started putting antiques and old knickknacks onto the third floor. Then the presence lessened. No one has ever felt threatened, though a few guests have not liked the idea of a ghost's being around. The problem with the light bulbs and candles is frustrating, but we've learned to live with it. Now we feel more protected than anything else, and so do the guests who have had encounters in their rooms, such as being tucked in or having their hair brushed out of their faces."

That feeling of being protected may have come partly from an incident that happened in 1991. At first it was startling, but at least whoever was responsible seemed to have the safety of the household in mind. Ken and Bonnie were alone in the inn and were expecting only one guest for the night. He was supposed to come by ten o'clock that evening, but didn't show. He called to say that if he got in at all, it would not be till midnight. They decided to retire for the night, leaving a key to the front door and to his room in an envelope beside the front door. A note on the door gave the location of the envelope. Included in the envelope were instructions for locking the second lock on the front door, which could only be locked from inside.

The room for their intended guest happened to be the one above the room that they were staying in at the time. Around midnight they heard the front door open, the sound of footsteps entering, and the sound of the front door's being locked. They heard footsteps of someone going toward the staircase and then going up the stairs. Then the upstairs room door opened and closed, and the sound of footsteps could be heard as someone entered the room.

Because the inside lock on the front door was not easy to properly secure, Bonnie got up to check it. It was firmly in place. She unlocked the front door and opened it to make certain that the note had been taken inside as well. The note was still there. She removed it and saw that the envelope was still where she had left it, with the keys inside.

"I went upstairs and checked the room where our guest was supposed to be. He wasn't there. He never did arrive that night, but somehow the doors were opened and then locked without the keys," Bonnie continued, "and then the front door had been secured from the inside.

"We feel more protected by our ghosts than anything else. Some of our guests hear about them and get excited—the ghosts add more to the experience of being here for the guests. We don't try to tell everyone about them, but we have no problem telling them if they ask."

The ghosts have only been seen to walk—they don't float or fly. Bonnie and Ken do all the flying—they are also pilots for commercial airlines. I asked Bonnie if she or Ken would tell their passengers about their experiences. Bonnie doesn't think it would make her passengers trust her any less if they knew she has actually seen a ghost or that her other business, the Seven Sisters Inn, had a couple of benign and even helpful spirits within. As it is, conflict-of-interest rules prohibit the two pilots from mentioning the Seven Sisters Inn to their passengers.

"But," Bonnie adds, "I wouldn't mind their knowing. I think they would trust me just the same."

The passengers will probably trust Bonnie and Ken more than ever. After all, the passengers will know that their pilot keeps a cool head when things get a little strange.

The Stanford Inn

Judging from the tasteful and well-mannered ghost who resides at the Stanford Inn in Bartow, the "good old days" may have been as full of gracious and genteel living as people claim to remember. As one drives the streets of Bartow toward 555 East Stanford Street, no speed limit signs are needed to remind one to slow down and admire the houses and gardens from Florida's past. The Stanford Inn is the crown jewel. Many words and phrases come to mind on one's first sight of the Inn; "beautifully restored" is one phrase, but it is inadequate. The tale behind those two words is the story of how Bob and Angie Clark, the proprietors, found a kindred spirit who turned out to be, well, a spirit.

The Clarks, who had long dreamed of owning an elegant bed-and-breakfast inn, closed on the house that was to become the Stanford Inn in January of 1997. Restoration work began immediately. While Angie stayed in Ft. Lauderdale to begin gathering furnishings, Bob and several workmen moved into the house and began demolishing the first floor. Soon there was barely enough first floor left to keep the second floor from crashing to the ground. No matter how hard they worked, Bob and his crew found themselves waking up at three o'clock every morning to...silence. No noise had startled them; they were simply awake and alert, and it would always take them about twenty minutes to get back to sleep.

As work progressed over the next few weeks, each of the men working occasionally heard footsteps, nearly always coming from the second floor even though no one was supposed to be up there. Voices were also heard from empty parts of the house. At night, footsteps often could be heard coming down the stairs from the second floor. The front door would open, apparently by itself, and then close after the sound of footsteps passed through it onto the wraparound porch. During this period of time, none of the men spoke to the others about what was happening.

At last Bob brought up the subject and told the others what he was hearing. The others were relieved to share what they had heard and to find that none of them was imagining things. Although once a worker had felt the breath of something unseen on the back of his neck and had been too startled to turn around and look, no one was frightened. Whatever the presence was, it was not at all threatening.

Around this time the former owner of the house came back to retrieve some furnishings he had left, and he asked Bob, "Have you seen or heard anything?"—implying something unusual. When asked about what had been going on, he elaborated: The activity was thought to be that of the ghost of Lee Meriwether, the mother of the actress of the same name.

The story was that Ms. Meriwether had lived in the house in its earlier days, preferring to stay in what is now the Cabbage Rose room on the second floor. Her marriage had not gone well. Her husband stayed in a downstairs bedroom. The footsteps now being heard nearly always originated in Ms. Meriwether's former bedroom, as did the voices.

As the work on the house continued, Lee (as she was now called) became more active in a mischievous and good-natured way. "Sometimes," Bob told me, "I would hear Angie's voice calling my name from upstairs. I would start to answer her and then remember that Angie was still in Ft. Lauderdale. Lee could imitate Angie perfectly. Once or twice one of the guys working with us would come up and tell me that Angie needed me upstairs for something, not knowing that Angie was away." Bob was not the only person who heard Lee calling his name; their fifteen-year-old son and many of the workers had had the same experience.

No tools were ever missing. No one was ever hurt. Everyone got used to Lee. There was even a little anticipation one night when her footsteps were heard on the stairway, going down as usual and then out the front door as it opened and closed. On the previous day, paper had been placed on the steps to protect them, and there was a lot of dust on the paper. Would they finally at least have her shoe size, since she was heard and never seen?

Unfortunately there were no prints in the dust. Then someone pointed out that the footsteps had sounded as if they were on wooden steps, not a paper-covered surface. It was as if the sounds had come from a past time before the paper had been put down. As Bob and Angie demonstrated the opening and closing of the front door, we heard the twin beeps of the door alarm sounding. "Whenever we hear the footsteps on the stairs and the opening of the door, the alarm never sounds. We don't know why."

Despite all the experiences that people in the house had had, Angie wasn't impressed when she returned and prepared to furnish and decorate. She heard no voices from empty rooms. She slept peacefully through the night without ever hearing phantom footsteps.

"We think that Lee was uncomfortable with only men in the house. She saw us doing all the work and had no idea what we were planning. We think she doesn't like change very much, especially where she used to live. She is very quiet when there are women in the house. We talked to the former owners about it. When there are only men in the house, her activity keeps stepping up, as if she is politely hinting that we should leave. When Angie came, it was a family house again and she seemed to like that.

"The people who had the house before us had bright colors like reds and canary yellows all over the house. When Angie started decorating, it was obvious that the house was going to be restored to the decor it had originally had. Lee became very quiet, as if she approved."

She was so quiet that Angie remained skeptical until some of their first guests astonished her by asking her about the ghost in the house. They were two men from Europe who had been staying in the Francesca suite upstairs. Not liking the sound of the air conditioner in the sunroom, they had gotten permission to move the mattress from the day bed into the main bedroom. They woke up that evening to see an attractive, dark-haired woman in white garb standing at the foot of the queen-sized bed and pointing toward the bathroom. Her hair was tied back in a bun. "She seemed to be trying to tell them something by her pointing. She was not stern or frightening in any way. They liked her but didn't know what she was trying to tell them. They described the whole experience as being very pleasant. Then she disappeared."

The Clarks had no pictures of Lee available to show their two guests. After they left, however, the Clarks found a photograph of some people who were guests at the house around 1906. To their surprise, the picture showed a number of women in flowing white dresses, nearly all of whom had their dark hair tied back in a style resembling a bun. The photo is still at the inn if anyone wishes to see it.

"I still didn't believe in ghosts then," laughed Angie, "but then I knew that something was definitely going on that I didn't understand."

Predictably, Lee and Angie crossed paths when Angie began furnishing and decorating the Cabbage Rose room, which was Lee's old bedroom. "I would put up drapes, and the next day one set would be on the floor. When I put them back up, another set would be on the floor the next morning," said Angie. "Sometimes I would turn on the lights and find that some light bulbs had been unscrewed. It would happen again later, but in a different chandelier." One night Angie slept in the Cabbage Rose room. "I sensed something over me. It was gentle, not scary. It wasn't the ceiling fan; it was closer than that."

"Lee must like the way things are now," said Bob. "We haven't had anything happen in months."

Some of the many guests at the Stanford Inn have heard of Lee and have even looked forward to one of her manifestations. Only two people have ever left on Lee's account, and no one knows if anything ever actually happened to them. "Now that we've had this conversation," Angie confided in me, "I'll bet some drapes are on the floor right now, and she's unscrewed some light bulbs."

I took the bet. "She's too polite. If she really likes the atmosphere here, why disrupt it so rudely?" We went upstairs to finish the tour, straight to the Cabbage Rose room. The drapes were in place and undisturbed. Angie reached for the light switch. All the lights came on within the chandelier.

I wasn't surprised at all. I know classy ladies when I see them. Or even if I can't.

Don CeSar

The diverse array of international influences on Florida is seen even in its ghost stories. Nowhere is this more evident than in the story of the Don CeSar Beach Resort.

A century ago in the late 1890s, Thomas Rowe was pursuing his education in London, England. It was there that he met Lucinda, the lovely Spanish diva who played the role of Maritana in Vincent Wallace's light opera of the same name. She was already living her dream of a career in opera. As they came to fall in love, they talked of his dream of building a grand hotel that would be a castle by the sea. He called her Maritana. She called him Don CeSar, after the hero of the opera she starred in.

Her parents called him unfit for her. Thomas and Lucinda were of different religious faiths. He was a student; she had a career. Her parents were also afraid that the closer their daughter drew to Thomas Rowe, the farther she drew from the life in opera that they had envisioned for her.

Don CeSar and Maritana were forced to meet secretly. They often did so near a fountain in London. Her parents' disapproval

The Don CeSar

only made Lucinda want to spend more time alone with Thomas, and finally she was forbidden to have any contact with him at all. It was made clear to Thomas that he had been cast out of the castle of her family.

He came to the United States, where he became a millionaire through dealings in Florida real estate. Letter after letter to Lucinda was returned unopened over a two-year period. The silence from abroad was finally broken by the news of Lucinda's death. However, she had been permitted to write him a letter from her deathbed. In part, it read, "Tom, my beloved Don CeSar: This life is only an intermediate plane. I leave it without regret and travel to a place where the swing of the pendulum does not bring pain. Time is infinite. I wait for you by our fountain to share our timeless love forever, Maritana."

In the 1920s Thomas Rowe moved to St. Petersburg. He had married by then, but the grand hotel that he began to build on the beach was a monument to Lucinda. Its architectural style was Moorish, recalling her Spanish heritage. The dominant feature of the courtyard was an elaborate fountain that reportedly looked just like the fountain in London where he and Lucinda had met so often.

In 1928, the hotel opened, and for twelve years Rowe actually lived within his dream. His quarters were on the fifth floor. He often mingled with the guests in the fifth floor dining room or the ground floor lobby until his death in 1940.

The military took over the hotel in 1941. In 1945 the Veterans Administration moved its offices there. Renovation after renovation took place, until by the 1960s the courtyard had been enclosed and the fountain demolished. That was enough for a citizens group that wanted the Don CeSar back. They were successful in their efforts. There was one last great renovation, and then the Don CeSar Beach Resort opened in 1973.

During the construction work of the early 1970s a thin, older man wearing an old-fashioned suit was seen many times walking around the construction site. Workers thought he was the manager or owner. They were told otherwise, but the man was still seen by hotel employees and guests after the gala reopening. Employees sometimes caught a glimpse of him in a mirror on the fifth floor hallway after stepping off the elevator although there was no one else in the hallway. Others, with hands full, would step onto an empty elevator and find that the button for the floor they wanted had already been pushed for them.

The man in the old-fashioned suit was seen over the years in the dining room, in the lobby, and in elevators. Guests were asked, "Are you enjoying your stay?" or "Did you enjoy your dinner?" before he disappeared into the crowd. Over and over, he fit the description of Thomas Rowe.

He even gave advice. When *Southern Bride* magazine came to use the hotel as a backdrop for a series of photos, Rowe appeared in the room of one of the editors. He advised her not to try to take a certain picture in a specific area of the hotel grounds. She tried anyway the following day, and a huge black crow ruined the session.

Tragedy often plagues those with the best of intentions. Rowe, made so unwelcome by others, lived his dreams of making others welcome in the most lavish of ways, perfect to the details. The sightings of someone who resembled him after his death suggested that he had devoted himself to perfecting Florida hospitality even after death. But his dreams proved as bitter for him as they were sweet to others.

A number of people were embarrassed and discomfited by the idea of the Don having a ghost roaming its hallways. There is a story that a manager actually saw Mr. Rowe once and used the opportunity to explain that Rowe's presence was becoming a problem for his own creation. Rowe agreed to confine himself to a suite of rooms on the fifth floor, which would be decorated in a style reminiscent of the 1930s. And he was not to manifest himself even in those rooms, if a guest wanted to use them.

Once again, Thomas Rowe had loved and lost.

After that meeting, in the 1980s, guests began asking about a second presence in the Don. It was an attractive woman in theatrical costume. Her dress was outrageously lavish and out of place, as if she had stepped off an opera stage. For a brief period, she was seen about the resort alone and then in the company of a thin man in an old-fashioned suit. There were a small number of sightings of the two in various places inside the hotel and then a last report of an oddly dressed couple, hand in hand, strolling down the beach of St. Pete.

They were slowly walking away from the Don, not looking back.

Could the woman have been Lucinda, come to convince her beloved to move on? *Time is infinite,* she had said. Those who thrive on conflict might say that she told him to choose between her and the hotel. I think that it was not so negative. I like to think that she had come to lure him to the most hospitable of all places.

I frequent St. Pete Beach. The sound of the gentle surf slowly brushes my tangled thoughts and feelings into something more manageable. I don't know in which direction Rowe and Lucinda went, but I think it was south. To the north is a crowd of buildings. The south beach loses itself in a jumbled horizon of sand and water.

The last time I was there, it was windy and cold, weather that had come from somewhere outside Florida and which would soon be won over by the sun. I was alone. I turned my back to the waves as they shattered in the cold wind. Towering over me was a castle by the sea, the offspring of Thomas and Lucinda.

Shivering next to an enclosed refreshment stand at the other edge of the beach was a young woman. She was employed by the Don. Thinking that I might be a hotel guest, she was determined to stay out there as long as I did, in case I cared for a hot chocolate or tea. She is one of the ones Thomas Rowe left behind and entrusted his dreams to.

We said hello to each other as I walked past her to begin the drive home. There was not much more to be learned about the spiritual state of Florida here. There were more tangible things to grapple with, such as the late afternoon traffic and the laundry.

I left her there alone on the windswept beach.

Epilogue

In my free time I still travel the length and breadth of Florida, gathering stories as other travelers gather souvenirs. Some of them are well known. Others have to be coaxed out of hiding. Some people laugh when I inquire about local legends; others nervously force themselves to laugh; still more shudder. Some say nothing. Oddly, no member of the Florida press has ever returned a call or note from me.

The people to whom I listen are citizens of a place called the Sunshine State, a nickname that ignores darkness. No state nickname can make the night go away. Nighttime comes as reliably as reminders of the darkness within our own souls, and of the forces around us that we don't fully understand. People both small and great have learned that we can't control everything well enough to bury something and to make certain that it stays that way.

There is conflict between the world we try to hide away and the one we all like to live in. There are secrets that haunt our nights, pounding on the doors of our wills and screaming to be let out. Our fears of those who haunt the darkness are partly kept at bay by those who haunt the sunshine. I have met them again and again. I look across Florida and they begin standing up in my memories. They are the shivering young woman who waited on me at the Don, even after being assured by me that it was not necessary. The old couple who had no time for bitterness over the past because they were busy giving thanks for what they had been given. The teacher whose devotion to his students ripples across time through their service to others. A mother who still grieves for her infant daughter despite the contempt of those who judged her.

They are the preacher at Denny's who let his food go cold while he made certain that the needs of his friends were met. A woman who doggedly preserved the lessons of the past and the history of her county, not knowing who would do so later. The teenager who could be trusted with the future because she had learned to be responsible for herself. And the little boy who was eager to share the lessons of his mother with those who needed them most.

I thought of them all as I drove eastward at sixty miles an hour down the highway into the night that was gathering around my home. The storm clouds ahead reminded me of the war between the world of darkness and that of light. There is no need for fear or hesitation. I knew then what I know now.

The darkness, however vast and full of terrors, is going to lose.

Bibliography

Falk Theater

Barrs, Jennifer. "Tampa Bay Haunts." *Tampa Tribune* (October 31, 1995).

Interview by author (anonymous source).

Lammers, Dirk. "Ghost Stories Light Up City's Youngish Past." *Tampa Tribune* (October 31, 1994).

Vogel, Chris, and Jennifer Barrs. "Strange Sightings Fuel Ghost Stories." *Tampa Tribune* (October 31, 1995).

Lake Worth Playhouse

"Community Theater Lore Full of Ghosts, Goof-ups." *Fort Lauderdale Sun-Sentinel* (September 30, 1985).

Hauck, Dennis William. *Haunted Places: The National Directory: A Guidebook to Ghostly Abodes, Sacred Sites, UFO Landings, and Other Supernatural Locations.* New York: The Penguin Group, 1996.

Interview by author (anonymous source).

Tampa Theatre

Barrs, Jennifer. "Tampa Bay Haunts." *Tampa Tribune* (October 31, 1995).

Hauck, Dennis William. *Haunted Places: The National Directory: A Guidebook to Ghostly Abodes, Sacred Sites, UFO Landings, and Other Supernatural Locations.* New York: The Penguin Group, 1996.

Interview by author (anonymous source).

Moore, Joyce Elson. *Haunt Hunter's Guide to Florida.* Sarasota, FL: Pineapple Press, 1998.

Norman, Michael, and Beth Scott. *Haunted America.* New York: Tom Doherty Associates, 1995.

Center Place

Interview by author (anonymous source).

Moore, Joyce Elson. *Haunt Hunter's Guide to Florida.* Sarasota, FL: Pineapple Press, 1998.

Daytona Playhouse

Kasko, Paul. "Community Spirits: Old Legends Say Ghosts Haunt Area." *Daytona Beach News-Journal* (October 31, 1987).

Moore, Joyce Elson. *Haunt Hunter's Guide to Florida.* Sarasota, FL: Pineapple Press, 1998.

A Night at the Roxy

Interview by author (anonymous source).

And Baby Makes Four

Interview by author (anonymous source).

Jennifer's Friend

Lapham, Dave. *Ghosts of St. Augustine.* Sarasota, FL: Pineapple Press, 1997.

The Quietest Neighbors

Lyle, Zannah. "Ghost Stories." *Tallahassee Democrat* (October 30, 1994): 1E.

Bill

Interview by author (anonymous source).

Charlotte

Interview by author (anonymous source).

The Scene of the Crime

Coole, Terri. "Murder Mystery Remains but the Ghost Has Vanished." *Orlando Sentinel* (October 30, 1992).

———. "They're Never Home Alone." *Orlando Sentinel* (October 31, 1995).

Sargent, Robert Jr. "Rumors Haunt House." *Orlando Sentinel* (October 31, 1998).

A Visit with Grandpa

Interview by author (anonymous source).

Fordham House

Johnson, Sandra, and Leora Sutton. *Ghosts, Legends, and Folklore of Old Pensacola.* Available from Pensacola Historical Society, Old Christ Church, 405 South Adams Street, Pensacola, FL 32501, 1990.

Electronic Ghost

Johnson, Sandra, and Leora Sutton. *Ghosts, Legends, and Folklore of Old Pensacola.* Available from Pensacola Historical Society, Old Christ Church, 405 South Adams Street,

Pensacola, FL 32501, 1990.

Party!

Lyle, Zannah. "Ghost Stories." *Tallahassee Democrat* (October 30, 1994): 1E.

Higgins' Haunted Home

Bair, Bill. "Families Share Spooky Secret." *The Ledger* (November 1, 1992).

———. "Jeepers Creepers." *The Ledger* (August 23, 1992).

———. "Paranormal Pursuit." *The Ledger* (September 20, 1992).

———. "They're Back." *The Ledger* (October 22, 1992).

Martin, Lydia. "Florida's Own Ghost Busters." *Miami Herald* (October 31, 1995): 1E.

UPI report. "Family Wants Out of 'Haunted' House." *Tampa Tribune* (August 28, 1992).

The Gray House of Pensacola

"Florida Is Alive with Ghosts." *Orlando Sentinel* (October 29, 1993).

Johnson, Sandra, and Leora Sutton. *Ghosts, Legends, and Folklore of Old Pensacola.* Available from Pensacola Historical Society, Old Christ Church, 405 South Adams Street, Pensacola, FL 32501, 1990.

"Old Haunts Spur New Round of Ghost Stories." *Orlando Sentinel* (October 31, 1985).

"Pensacola's Ghosts Ready for Halloween." *Miami Herald* (October 31, 1985): 2D.

There Goes the Neighborhood

Cain, Suzy, and Dianne Thompson Jacoby. *A Ghostly Experience.* St. Augustine, FL: Tour St. Augustine, Inc.

"Ghost Stories Fuel Business." *Tampa Tribune* (September 3, 1996).

Lowe, Tom. "In Search of Oldest City's Ghosts." *Orlando Sentinel* (October 26, 1997).

Old Leon County Jail

"Book on Florida Ghosts in the Works." *Tallahassee Democrat* (October 30, 1994).

Hauck, Dennis William. *Haunted Places: The National Directory: A Guidebook to Ghostly Abodes, Sacred Sites, UFO Landings, and Other Supernatural Locations.* New York: The Penguin Group, 1996.

Reaver, J. Russell, ed. *Florida Folktales.* Gainesville, FL: University Presses, 1987.

Old Bradford House

Bassett, Stacey. "Gunning for Fun: History Repeats Itself in Ma Barker Day Reenactment." *Ocala Star-Banner* (January 11, 1998).

Burnett, Gene M. *Florida's Past: People and Events That Shaped the State,* Vol. 3. Sarasota, FL: Pineapple Press, 1986.

Gyllenhaal, Anders. "Rattle of Guns Returns to Sleepy Florida

Town Where Ma Barker Died."
Miami Herald (January 19, 1985).

Hauck, Dennis William.
Haunted Places: The National Directory: A Guidebook to Ghostly Abodes, Sacred Sites, UFO Landings, and Other Supernatural Locations. New York: The Penguin Group, 1996.

http://www.oklahombres.org/barker1.htm.

http://www.starbanner.com/Headliners/1998/Barker011198.html.

http://www.starbanner.com/History/Barker.html.

Maeder, Jay. "Ma Barker: Still Dead After All These Years." *Miami Herald* (February 24, 1985).

See Rollie Run

"Halloween Makes Gamble Place Ghosts Extra Lively." *Orlando Sentinel* (October 18, 1992).

Interview by author (anonymous source).

Smith, Jessi Jackson. "2000: Gamble Place in the New Millennium." *Arts & Sciences Magazine*, The Museum of Arts & Sciences, Daytona, FL (Winter 2000).

Ste. Claire, Dana. "Gamble Place: Turn-of-the-Century Florida Preserved." *Arts & Sciences Magazine*, The Museum of Arts & Sciences, Daytona, FL (Autumn 1989).

———. "James N. Gamble: Florida's First Winter Resident."
Arts & Sciences Magazine, The Museum of Arts & Sciences, Daytona, FL (Autumn 1990).

———. "Once Upon a Time on Spruce Creek." *Arts & Sciences Magazine*, The Museum of Arts & Sciences, Daytona, FL (Spring 1991).

———. "Recollections of the Orange: The Gamble Place Citrus Packing Barn." *Arts & Sciences Magazine*, The Museum of Arts & Sciences, Daytona, FL (Summer 1991).

———. "Snow White Fantasy Landscape Discovered." *Arts & Sciences Magazine*, The Museum of Arts & Sciences, Daytona, FL (Summer 1993).

Stewart, Laura, and Susanne Hupp. *Historic Homes of Florida.* Sarasota, FL: Pineapple Press, 1995.

"Volusia is Haunted by Ghostly Stories." *Orlando Sentinel* (October 19, 1997).

Reaching Out

Johnson, Sandra, and Leora Sutton. *Ghosts, Legends, and Folklore of Old Pensacola.* Available from Pensacola Historical Society, Old Christ Church, 405 South Adams Street, Pensacola, FL 32501, 1990.

The Empty Bathtub

Covington, James W. *The Story of Southwestern Florida*, Vol 1. New York: Lewis Historical Publishing Co., 1957.

Garrison, Webb. *A Treasury of Florida Tales*. Nashville: Rutledge Hill Press, 1989.

The Koreshan Unity Settlement (Koreshan State Historic Site brochure), Estero, FL.

McIver, Stuart B. *Dreamers, Schemers, and Scalawags: The Florida Chronicles*, Vol 1. Sarasota, FL: Pineapple Press, 1994.

Stewart, Laura, and Susanne Hupp. *Historic Homes of Florida*. Sarasota, FL: Pineapple Press, 1995.

Castillo de San Marcos

Cain, Suzy, and Dianne Thompson Jacoby. *A Ghostly Experience*. St. Augustine, FL: Tour St. Augustine, Inc., 1997.

Hauck, Dennis William. *Haunted Places: The National Directory: A Guidebook to Ghostly Abodes, Sacred Sites, UFO Landings, and Other Supernatural Locations*. New York: The Penguin Group, 1996.

Interview by author (anonymous source).

Moore, Joyce Elson. *Haunt Hunter's Guide to Florida*. Sarasota, FL: Pineapple Press, 1998.

Lady's Walk

Johnson, Sandra, and Leora Sutton. *Ghosts, Legends, and Folklore of Old Pensacola*. Available from Pensacola Historical Society, Old Christ Church, 405 South Adams Street, Pensacola, FL 32501, 1990.

Seahorse Key

McCarthy, M. Kevin. *Florida Lighthouses*. Gainesville, FL: University of Florida Press, 1990.

Villa Paula House

Dunlop, Beth. "Old Haunts: When it Comes to Architecture, Ghosts Seem to Prefer the Exotic." *Miami Herald* (October 31, 1988): 1C.

Hauck, Dennis William. *Haunted Places: The National Directory: A Guidebook to Ghostly Abodes, Sacred Sites, UFO Landings, and Other Supernatural Locations*. New York: The Penguin Group, 1996.

Norman, Michael, and Beth Scott. *Historic Haunted America*. New York: Tor Books, 1996.

"Postal Clerk Wins Deed to Villa with Haunted Past." *Orlando Sentinel* (May 13, 1985).

Watcher

Brown, Loren G. "Totch." *Totch: A Life in the Everglades*. Gainesville, FL: University Press of Florida, 1993.

Bruce, Annette J. *Tellable Cracker Tales*. Sarasota, FL: Pineapple Press, 1966.

Burnett, Gene M. *Florida's Past: People and Events that Shaped the State*, Vol. 1. Sarasota, FL: Pineapple Press, Inc., 1986.

Covington, James W. *The Story of Southwestern Florida*, Vol. 1. New York: Lewis Historical Publishing Co., 1957.

Douglas, Marjory Stoneman. *The Everglades: River of Grass*, 50th Anniv. Ed. Sarasota, FL: Pineapple Press, 1997.

Historic Smallwood Store pamphlet. Available inside the store and at the Everglades Visitor Center.

McIver, Stuart B. *Murder in the Tropics: The Florida Chronicles*, Vol. 2. Sarasota, FL: Pineapple Press, Inc., 1995.

———. *True Tales of the Everglades*. Miami, FL: Florida Flair Books, 1989.

Simmons, Glen, and Laura Ogden. *Gladesmen: Gator Hunters, Moonshiners, and Skiffers*. Gainesville, FL: University Press of Florida, 1998.

Tebeau, Charlton. *Florida's Last Frontier: The History of Collier County*. Coral Gables, FL: University of Miami Press, 1957.

———. *The Story of the Chokoloskee Bay Country: With the Reminiscences of Pioneer C. S. "Ted" Smallwood*. Coral Gables, FL: University of Miami Press, 1955.

Old Christ Church in Pensacola

Johnson, Sandra, and Leora Sutton. *Ghosts, Legends, and Folklore of Old Pensacola*. Available from Pensacola Historical Society, Old Christ Church, 405 South Adams Street, Pensacola, FL 32501, 1990.

Moore, Joyce Elson. *Haunt Hunter's Guide to Florida*. Sarasota, FL: Pineapple Press, Inc., 1998.

Tarpon Springs

Burnett, Gene M. *Florida's Past: People and Events that Shaped the State*, Vol. 1. Sarasota, FL: Pineapple Press, Inc., 1986.

Interview by author (anonymous source).

Miller, Bill. *Tampa Triangle: Dead Zone*. St. Petersburg, FL: Ticket to Adventure, Inc., 1997.

"Weeping Icon of St. Nicholas" (pamphlet). Available at the Cathedral of St. Nicholas.

St. Paul's Episcopal Church

Interview by author (anonymous source).

46 Avenida Menendez

Cain, Suzy, and Dianne Thompson Jacoby. *A Ghostly Experience*. St. Augustine, FL: Tour St. Augustine, Inc., 1997.

Hauck, Dennis William. *Haunted Places: The National Directory: A Guidebook to Ghostly Abodes, Sacred Sites, UFO Landings, and Other Supernatural Locations*. New York: The Penguin Group, 1996.

Interview by author (anonymous source).

Lapham, Dave. *Ghosts of St. Augustine.* Sarasota, FL: Pineapple Press, Inc., 1997.

Moore, Joyce Elson. *Haunt Hunter's Guide to Florida.* Sarasota, FL: Pineapple Press, Inc., 1998.

Fireside Restaurant

Interview by author (anonymous source).

"Old-Time Spooks Familiar Frights in Brooksville." *Tampa Tribune* (October 31, 1993).

Ashley's

Caporale, Patricia. "Though Spirited Guests Stayed, Host Says It Was No Nightmare." *Orlando Sentinel* (October 31, 1992).

Hauck, Dennis William. *Haunted Places: The National Directory: A Guidebook to Ghostly Abodes, Sacred Sites, UFO Landings, and Other Supernatural Locations.* New York: The Penguin Group, 1996.

Interview by author (anonymous source).

Moore, Joyce Elson. *Haunt Hunter's Guide to Florida.* Sarasota, FL: Pineapple Press, Inc., 1998.

Myers, Arthur. *The Ghostly Register.* Chicago, IL: Contemporary Books, 1986.

Owens, Darryl E. "Florida Is Alive with Ghosts." *Orlando Sentinel* (October 29, 1993).

Pizza Hut

Interview by author (anonymous source).

Homestead Restaurant

History of the Homestead Restaurant (printed menu).

Interview by author (anonymous sources).

Biglow-Helms House

Interview by author (anonymous source).

Lammers, Dirk. "Ghost Stories Light Up City's Youngish Past." *Tampa Tribune* (October 31, 1994).

Vogel, Chris, and Jennifer Barrs. "Strange Sightings Fuel Ghost Stories." *Tampa Tribune* (October 31, 1995).

Community Development Corporation

"Agency Staff Vows to Leave 'Haunted' Office." *Miami Herald* (June 14, 1982): 7A.

DeBary Hall

Burnett, Gene M. *Florida's Past: People and Events That Shaped the State*, Vol. 2. Sarasota, FL: Pineapple Press, Inc., 1986.

"Don't Believe in Ghosts? A Visit to Debary Hall Could Change Your Mind." *Orlando Sentinel* (October 24, 1997).

The Muse of Maitland

"A-Haunting We Will Go."

Orlando Sentinel (October 27, 1991).

Interview by author (anonymous source).

Moore, Joyce Elson. *Haunt Hunter's Guide to Florida.* Sarasota, FL: Pineapple Press, Inc., 1998.

"Though Spirited Guest Stayed, Host Says It Was No Nightmare." *Orlando Sentinel* (October 31, 1992).

St. Petersburg High School

Interview by author (anonymous source).

SPHS Revisited (videotape). St. Petersburg, FL: Media Concepts, Inc., 1994.

Vogel, Chris, and Jennifer Barrs. "Strange Sightings Fuel Ghost Stories." *Tampa Tribune* (October 31, 1995).

Skyway Bridge Hitchhiker

Dymond, Richard. "Ghost Stories and Phobias Ride the Skyway Bridge, Too." *Bradenton Herald.*

Hauck, Dennis William. *Haunted Places: The National Directory: A Guidebook to Ghostly Abodes, Sacred Sites, UFO Landings, and Other Supernatural Locations.* New York: The Penguin Group, 1996.

Miller, Bill. *Tampa Triangle: Dead Zone.* St. Petersburg, FL: Ticket to Adventure, Inc., 1997.

Vogel, Chris, and Jennifer Barrs. "Strange Sightings Fuel

Ghost Stories." *Tampa Tribune* (October 31, 1995).

"Welcome to the Dead Zone." *Bradenton Herald* (December 8, 1996): F1.

Spook Hill

"Spook Hill: Where 'Up' is 'Down' and 'Down' is 'Up.'" *Miami Herald* (November 23, 1984).

Vogel, Chris, and Jennifer Barrs. "Strange Sightings Fuel Ghost Stories." *Tampa Tribune* (October 31, 1995).

"Yes, Something Really IS Weird at Spook Hill." *Bradenton Herald* (November 19, 1990).

Jessie May

Barrs, Jennifer. "Tampa Bay Haunts." *Tampa Tribune* (October 31, 1995).

Harger, Cindy. "Old-Time Spooks Familiar Frights in Brooksville." *Tampa Tribune* (October 31, 1993): 1.

Interview by author (anonymous source).

Jackson, Virginia. *Heritage Museum: May-Stringer House* (brochure). Available onsite. Brooksville, FL, 1994.

———. "History of the Stringer House." Heritage Museum: May-Stringer House. Available onsite. Brooksville, FL, 1995.

The Phantom Civil War Patrol

Johnson, Sandra, and Leora Sutton. *Ghosts, Legends, and Folklore of Old Pensacola.* Available from Pensacola Historical Society, Old Christ Church, 405 South Adams Street, Pensacola, FL 32501, 1990.

The Phantoms of Fort Taylor

Bellido, Susana. "Civil War Haunt's Walls Have Fears." *Miami Herald* (October 26, 1994).

Fort Zachary Taylor State Historic Site, Florida Department of Environmental Protection, Division of Recreation and Parks (brochure), Rev. 5/97.

"Happy Halloween." *Florida Times-Union* (October 31, 1997): 1B.

Interview by author (anonymous source).

Long, Phil. "Florida's Ghosts Are a Restless, Helpful Lot." *Bradenton Herald* (October 31, 1995).

Moore, Joyce Elson. *Haunt Hunter's Guide to Florida.* Sarasota, FL: Pineapple Press, Inc., 1998.

Fort Clinch

"Happy Halloween." *Florida Times-Union* (October 31, 1997).

Interview by author (anonymous source).

Long, Phil. "Florida's Ghosts Are a Restless, Helpful Lot." *Bradenton Herald* (October 31, 1995).

Moore, Joyce Elson. *Haunt Hunter's Guide to Florida.* Sarasota, FL: Pineapple Press, Inc., 1998.

A Confederate Funeral

Interview by author (anonymous source).

Magnolia Hall

Interview by author (anonymous source).

Biltmore

Bermudez, Raul A. "Tour Miami's Most Luxurious Haunt." *Miami Herald* (April 19, 1998).

"Biltmore Hotel Offers Some Ghostly Delights." *Miami Herald* (October 30, 1994).

Burnett, Gene M. *Florida's Past: People and Events That Shaped the State,* Vol. 3. Sarasota, FL: Pineapple Press, Inc., 1986.

Dunlop, Beth. "Old Haunts: When it Comes to Architecture, Ghosts Seem to Prefer the Exotic." *Miami Herald* (October 31, 1988): 1C.

Hauck, Dennis William. *Haunted Places: The National Directory: A Guidebook to Ghostly Abodes, Sacred Sites, UFO Landings, and Other Supernatural Locations.* New York: The Penguin Group, 1996.

Interview by author (anonymous source).

Moore, Joyce Elson. *Haunt Hunter's Guide to Florida.* Sarasota, FL: Pineapple Press, Inc., 1998.

Perez, Ivonne. "Ghost Stories Just Won't Die." *Miami Herald* (September 24, 1999).

"Phantoms of the Biltmore." *Fort Lauderdale Sun-Sentinel* (October 26, 1986).

"Things That Go Bump." *Orlando Sentinel* (September 30, 1985).

Whited, Charles. "New Paint Job Puts Some Life in Old Biltmore." *Miami Herald* (September 28, 1986): 1B.

Boca Raton Resort and Club

Harris, John. "Ghost of Chambermaid Tidies Guest Rooms at Boca Resort." *Miami Herald* (Boca Raton edition) (October 31, 1998).

Interview by author (anonymous source).

McIver, Stuart B. *Dreamers, Schemers, and Scalawags: The Florida Chronicles*, Vol. 1. Sarasota, FL: Pineapple Press, Inc., 1994.

Casablanca Inn

Cain, Suzy, and Dianne Thompson Jacoby. *A Ghostly Experience.* St. Augustine, FL: Tour St. Augustine, Inc., 1997.

Estes, Jacque. "Take Tour, Then Tell Your Own Ghost Stories." *Daytona Beach News-Journal* (May 26, 1999).

"A Ghostly Tale" (http://www.casablancainn.com/ghost.html).

Hauck, Dennis William. *Haunted Places: The National Directory: A Guidebook to Ghostly Abodes, Sacred Sites, UFO Landings, and Other Supernatural Locations.* New York: The Penguin Group, 1996.

"In Search of Oldest City's Ghosts." *Orlando Sentinel* (October 26, 1997).

Interview by author (anonymous source).

Lapham, Dave. *Ghosts of St. Augustine.* Sarasota, FL: Pineapple Press, Inc., 1997.

Thurwachter, Mary. "Tired of the Same Old Haunts? Try St. Augustine." *Palm Beach Post* (October 31, 1999).

Cassadaga

"A-Haunting We Will Go." *Orlando Sentinel* (October 27, 1991).

Moore, Joyce Elson. *Haunt Hunter's Guide to Florida.* Sarasota, FL: Pineapple Press, Inc., 1998.

"Though Spirited Guest Stayed, Host Says It Was No Nightmare." *Orlando Sentinel* (October 31, 1992).

Herlong Mansion

Bauer, Gerri. "Double Occupancy—Hotel Ghosts a Spirited Bunch." *Daytona Beach*

Sunday News-Journal (October 27, 1996).

Betancort, Mariel. "Explore Florida's Past with *Haunt Hunter's Guide*." *Tallahassee Democrat* (October 28, 1998): 2D.

Fridl, Melanie. "Boooooo." *Tampa Tribune* (October 29, 1992).

"Ghost Tales Are Just a Small Part of Micanopy's Charm." *Miami Herald* (October 6, 1996).

Interview by author (anonymous source).

Martin, Lydia. "Florida's Own Ghost Busters." *Miami Herald* (October 31, 1995): 1E.

"Micanopy Mansion a Pleasant Haunt." *Tampa Tribune* (November 24, 1995).

Moore, Joyce Elson. *Haunt Hunter's Guide to Florida*. Sarasota, FL: Pineapple Press, Inc., 1998.

"Mysteries Call Old Mansion Their Home." *Miami Herald* (September 1, 1997).

Stewart, Laura, and Susanne Hupp. *Historic Homes of Florida*. Sarasota, FL: Pineapple Press, Inc., 1995.

Seven Sisters Inn

Fridl, Melanie. "Boooooo." *Tampa Tribune* (October 29, 1992).

Interview by author (anonymous source).

Stewart, Laura, and Susanne Hupp. *Historic Homes of Florida*. Sarasota, FL: Pineapple Press, Inc., 1995.

The Stanford Inn

Interview by author (anonymous source).

The Stanford Inn (brochure), Bartow, FL.

Don CeSar

Barrs, Jennifer. "Tampa Bay Haunts." *Tampa Tribune* (October 31, 1995).

Bauer, Gerri. "Double Occupancy—Hotel Ghosts a Spirited Bunch." *Daytona Beach Sunday News-Journal* (October 27, 1996).

Hauck, Dennis William. *Haunted Places: The National Directory: A Guidebook to Ghostly Abodes, Sacred Sites, UFO Landings, and Other Supernatural Locations*. New York: The Penguin Group, 1996.

Miller, Bill. *Tampa Triangle: Dead Zone*. St. Petersburg, FL: Ticket to Adventure, Inc., 1997.

Young, Jane H. *The Don CeSar Story*. St. Petersburg, FL: Partnership Press, 1974.

Index

If you enjoyed reading this book, here are some other books from Pineapple Press on related topics. For a complete catalog, write to Pineapple Press, P.O. Box 3899, Sarasota, FL 34230 or call 1-800-PINEAPL (746-3275). Or visit our website at www.pineapplepress.com.

Death in Bloodhound Red by Virginia Lanier. Jo Beth Sidden, who trains bloodhounds for search-and-rescue missions, must prove her innocence when she's suspected of murder. ISBN 1-56164-076-X (hb)

The Florida Chronicles by Stuart B. McIver. A series offering true-life sagas of the notable and notorious characters throughout history who have given Florida its distinctive flavor. **Volume 1** *Dreamers, Schemers and Scalawags* ISBN 1-56164-155-3 (pb); **Volume 2** *Murder in the Tropics* ISBN 1-56164-079-4 (hb)

Florida Portrait by Jerrell Shofner. Packed with hundreds of photos, this word-and-picture album traces the history of Florida from the Paleo-Indians to the rampant growth of the late twentieth century. ISBN 1-56164-121-9 (pb)

Florida's Past Volumes 1, 2, and 3 by Gene Burnett. Collected essays from Burnett's "Florida's Past" columns in *Florida Trend* magazine, plus some original writings not found elsewhere. Burnett's easygoing style and his sometimes surprising choice of topics make history good reading. **Volume 1** ISBN 1-56164-115-4 (pb); **Volume 2** ISBN 1-56164-139-1 (pb); **Volume 3** ISBN 1-56164-117-0 (pb)

Ghosts of St. Augustine by Dave Lapham. The unique and often turbulent history of America's oldest city is told in twenty-four spooky stories that cover four hundred years' worth of ghosts. ISBN 1-56164-123-5 (pb)

Ghosts of the Carolina Coasts by Terrance Zepke. Taken from real-life occurrences and Carolina Lowcountry lore, these thirty-two spine-tingling ghost stories take place in prominent historic structures of the region. ISBN 1-56164-175-8 (pb)

Guide to Florida Historical Walking Tours by Roberta Sandler. Put on your walking shoes and experience the heart of Florida's people, history, and architecture as you take a healthful, entertaining stroll through 32 historic neighborhoods. ISBN 1-56164-105-7 (pb)

Haunt Hunter's Guide to Florida by Joyce Elson Moore. Discover the general history and "haunt" history of numerous sites around the state where ghosts reside. ISBN 1-56164-150-2 (pb)

Historic Homes of Florida by Laura Stewart and Susanne Hupp. Seventy-four notable dwellings throughout the state—all open to the public—tell the human side of history. Each is illustrated by H. Patrick Reed or Nan E. Wilson. ISBN 1-56164-085-9 (pb)

Historical Traveler's Guide to Florida by Eliot Kleinberg. More than sixty travel destinations in Florida of great (and not so great) historical significance, all in the spirit of fun and exploration. ISBN 1-56164-122-7 (pb)

Houses of St. Augustine by David Nolan. A history of the city told through its buildings, from the earliest coquina structures, through the colonial and Victorian times, to the modern era. Color photographs and original watercolors. ISBN 1-56164-069-7 (hb); 1-56164-075-1 (pb)

Mystery in the Sunshine State edited by Stuart Kaminsky. An enticing selection of Florida mystery fare from some of Florida's most notable writers. ISBN 1-56164-185-5 (pb)

Power in the Blood by Michael Lister. Cop-turned-priest John Jordan investigates the death of inmate Ike Johnson in the Florida Panhandle's toughest prison. ISBN 1-56164-137-5 (hb)

The Return by Mark T. Mustian. From Miami to the streets of Brazil, ex-priest Michael Mason follows a trail that could prove the second coming of Christ. A thriller of a page turner by a first-time author. ISBN 1-56164-190-1 (hb)

Southeast Florida Pioneers by William McGoun. Meet the pioneers of the Palm Beach area, the Treasure Coast, and Lake Okeechobee in this collection of well-told, fact-filled stories from the 1690s to the 1990s. ISBN 1-56164-157-X (hb)